I AM YOUR
BROTHER

JAIMY REYNOLDS

Jaimy Reynolds
Jaimyreynolds@mywebsite.com

Book Cover & Interior Design by:
Alaka Oladimeji B.

DEDICATION

I would like to thank my Lord and Savior Jesus Christ. I want to dedicate and give a special thanks to my little brother Jaicy Reynolds, for allowing me to live with him and finish the book at my own pace. I thank God for blessing me to have a blood brother like you. I also would like to personally thank old school Bobby Lawrence for the love and support during the writing process. To my childhood friend Don Scott for the love & support, more importantly by being a great example to learn from.

Also, I would like to dedicate this to my mother Elinda Bradshaw, my father Kenneth Reynolds, my sister's Jessica Reynolds, Andrea Whitlock & Kiya Reynolds, step mother Alisa Puckett, Ginger Smith, Brandon Harris, Kevin Ford, Melvin Wright, Travis Mcfadgon, Laquintas Johnson & Chris Hall.

To every person that I ever crossed paths with and made a impact in my life. To all of my nieces and nephew's. To all of my Reynolds and Bradshaw family. To my close friends. To the East side of Arlington Texas. To every person whoever believed and supported me. To every person who makes this world a better place. To every person who battles depression and loneliness. To the future generation. To the single parents who work hard to provide. To every person who strives to better themselves. To every person who loves beyond skin color. To every messenger who feels like they live on a island. To my favorite music artist kid Cudi and Andre 3000. To every woman whoever loved me at anytime of their life. To everyone who is reading this. This is for you.

TABLE OF CONTENTS

INTRODUCTION

I believe that I was supposed to see, feel, sacrifice and experience everything that I have in order to write this book.

Over the coarse of my adult life this particular story has slowly but surely been puzzled together in my mind. In my minds eye, this is more that just a story, it is my calling. This world I have created has taken on its own personality and has become larger than life, larger than the man writing it.

Once I felt in my spirit that it was time to share my vision in book form, I stepped out on faith and went all in.

When I fully understood the urgency to share these people with the world, I gave up my full time job, sold off most of my possessions gave up anything and everything that could have stood on the way of focusing on my craft and completing this work. I hope you are as moved by this story as I was writing it. And we here are..

Chapter

I

Flashback

Seven walks towards the emergency room exit in a state of shock. His clothes and parts of his skin are painted in blood. Just as he enters the rotating doors from inside the building, a police officer enters from the outside. He makes eye contact with the officer who wore an eye patch over his left eye. Seven tightens his grip on his backpack, while mentally preparing himself to take off running. The police officer remained inside the rotating doors to circle back around. His one eye stayed glued on Seven as his figure faded from the horizon.

Seven picks up his tempo once out of sight of the police officer. He makes his way to the nearest bus stop where he contemplates his next move. His options are limited from his cell phone being dead. He snaps out of a staring daze once the bus came to a complete stop in front of him. He receives stares all the way to the back of the bus from his bloody attire. He tightly grips his backpack as if his life depends on it; then puts on a pair of headphones that connects to his mini ipod. The soothing jazz of Miles Davis blended with life outside the moving bus, like a movie scene he wished could be a dream.

Seven tips the bus driver and begins to walk in the midnight hour. He never shows up to his girlfriend's house unannounced, but due to the situation he makes the move. When approaching her front door, he noticed an unfamiliar truck parked in the drive way. One set of knocks turned into two set of knocks. She never took this long to answer the door. His patience was being tested while his mind began to assume the worst. Finally, she partially opens the door enough to where he could see her pretty face and disturbance in her eyes.

"Seven, what's going on, why didn't you call?" "My phone is dead," he answers back. "Oh my God!" "Are you okay," she nervously speaks after seeing the blood stains on his clothes. He dismisses her concern and asks why she was standing in front of the door. Her voice trembles with uncertainty. "I can't let you in right now, it's not a good time." He slightly grins while looking into her eyes. "Who's truck is that in the drive way?" She pauses before answering, "lets just talk tomorrow please, it's already late." His body temperature rises while remaining calm, "if you don't let me in this door, you are going to see another side of me that you have never seen before." "Please don't do this, I tried to talk to you the other day but you were busy," she replies.

Seven pushes the door open with one hand and gently stiff arms his way in with the other hand. He walks into the living room and sees another man standing there with half his clothes on, looking as if he just saw a ghost. They both stood there looking at each other like an old wild west stand-off between two gun-slingers. The energy of fear circulated the room from not knowing the next move of the calm and collective Seven. He turns around and walks into the kitchen. He opens the refrigerator door and takes out a bottle of wine, pops the top and drinks from the bottle. The other two stood there fearfully stunned and confused.

Seven takes his last sip before putting the bottle back in the refrigerator. He walks smoothly into the living room while the other two watch him from behind. He takes off his backpack and sits down on the couch. He turns the television on with the remote control and turns the channel to the animal planet. His girlfriend and the half-naked man stood their puzzled before he rushes to put on his shirt and shoes while stumbling all over the place. He dashes out the front door and cranks up his truck; burning rubber loud enough to wake the neighborhood.

She walks slowly into the living room while watching the back of Sevens head. She curved around the couch in slow motion before sitting at a distance. She stares at the side of his face before speaking, "he's just a friend." Seven tunes her out while listening to the

• • •

narrator's voice on Animal Planet speak of the introvert ways of the lone wolf. He slowly lifted his backpack and placed it in between his feet; then befins to unzip the black backpack.

With a sorrowful tone in her voice, "I'm sorry for what's happening, I'm so confused right now." He looks in her eyes and replies, "Only if you could have been a little more patient with me?" She jumps to her defense, what does that mean?" I tried to wait, I tried to be patient, it's like you changed." Who quits their great paying job, runs away from life, and throws everything they worked for away?"

In the mist of her speaking, Seven reaches into the backpack and pulls out stacks of money and sets it on the coffee table. He continues to reach inside and pull out handfuls of money wrapped in paper bands. Her mouth drops from seeing all the money being piled up on her table. Seven stops handling the money for a moment and watches the lone wolf attack its prey in the white winter snow, while ravishing the throat of his its soon to be food. He stays tuned in on the lone wolf while putting the money back in the backpack. He slips out a $100 dollar bill and places it on the coffee table. "This is for you and your new friend, dinner is on me."

Once all the money was back inside the backpack, he stands to his feet and leaves her side. He walks into her bedroom for a moment and comes back out with a shirt of his. He takes off the red stained shirt and stuffs it inside the backpack, then puts on the clean shirt. She never got tired of looking at his chiseled body. It would be her last time to do so as he walks out the front door without saying goodbye. He takes a deep breath before walking back towards the bus stop. The dark night was illuminated by the full moon and bright scattered stars. Not once did he look back.

● ● ●

Chapter

2

How It All Got Started

LOCATION: THE MELTING POT LOUNGE

Lead Singer: Thank you once again ladies and gentlemen, we are your live cover band for tonight, "A Chosen Few" (claps of satisfaction from the mellow crowd). And don't forget its open mic tonight, so the floor can be yours. The mic is set, feel free to come up and do whatever you feel. The kitchen and the bar are still open. So let's eat, drink, and be merry.

A romantic ambience inside the lounge gave a grown and sexy feel. A man named Seven sits alone in a curved booth and peeps out the scene. The sound of pool balls clash at a distance, just before a young waitress arrives.

WAITRESS: And here is your drink sir.

SEVEN: I thank you.

WAITRESS: I have never seen you in here before.

SEVEN: This is my first time.

WAITRESS: So what brings you out to tonight, if you don't mind me asking?

SEVEN: It's my birthday, so I just decided to get out of the house and come listen to some music.

WAITRESS: Well happy birthday to you!

SEVEN: Well thank you.

WAITRESS: You just hold on one second, I have something for you.

SEVEN: It's okay, you don't have to get me anything. Your positive energy is enough for me.

She appreciates his sentiment with a smile, then turns and leaves for the kitchen. Seven turns his attention to the live band while taking a sip of his drink. It wasn't long before the waitress returns with a lit candle sticking out of a piece of cake.

WAITRESS: I hope you like chocolate cake.

SEVEN: You are one cool lady.. and yes, I do like chocolate cake.

WAITRESS: Good, but before you blow out the candle, you have to make a wish. You never know, your wish just might come true.

Seven wasn't really up for blowing out any candles or bringing attention to himself, but the natural charmer went along with her command. He had a thing for good hearts, there was no way he was not going to deny someone who went out of there way for him. He closes his eyes for a quick second and blows out the candle. He shakes her hand and thanks her before she carries on and leaves him back into his comfort zone. In just moments later, a strange woman who looked like she belonged on somebody's TV approached from his side. His automatic attraction to her momentarily had him speechless.

DESTINY: Would you mind if I sat down for a moment?

SEVEN: ... No I don't mind, go right ahead.

DESTINY: Are you the light?

SEVEN: Excuse me..

Destiny: Do you have a light?

Seven: I'm sorry, no ma'am I don't.

Destiny: Hmm courteous I see.. but okay, I guess. I don't smoke but I am tonight.

SEVEN: That's interesting, because I don't drink, but I am tonight.

DESTINY: aw poor baby.. you want me to be your counselor for a moment, so you can tell me what's bothering you? I won't judge you. And since you are easy on the eyes, it will be free of charge.

SEVEN: I'm flattered coming from such a beautiful woman like yourself.

DESTINY: Beauty can be overrated don't you think?

SEVEN: It can be, depending on your definition of Beauty. What makes you believe there is something bothering me?

DESTINY: (Leaning forward to make direct eye contact) I looked deep into your eyes, and those never lie, unless you are really good.

SEVEN: Oh is that so.. when you speak of, "unless you are really good," do you mean good as in.. when asking me if I have a light, your true intention was to see if I was to be wearing a ring?

DESTINY: (Leans in a little closer with a sparkle in her eye) Yes. That type of good.

Destiny breaks the connection between the two and leans back from Seven. She swipes her finger across a corner of the chocolate icing and then licks it off. She stands up from the booth with her eyes still engaged in his. She drifts off into the crowd while he began weaving his head through the human traffic to locate her. Seven snaps out of a daze and takes another sip of his drink. He looks at the swiped part of the icing that was taken without permission. He shakes his head while grinning of her wittiness. He picks up the piece of cake and bites the part that she wiped off. The mingling of the lounge was interrupted by the sound of a microphone being taken off the stand and lightly tapped. The voice of the intriguing woman began to speak. Seven stopped chewing once hearing her voice. He looks towards the band but cannot visually see her from where he is sitting. All he can hear is her voice throughout the lounge. Her innocent but yet sexy voice serenades the place. She turns back and looks at the band.

DESTINY: Can you play something with a real light tone, something I can talk to.

Hello good people, my name is Destiny June. I won't be taking much of your time, but something just crossed my mind.

A mellow tone from the band fills the room. She steps closer to the mic and patiently speaks.

"I see something in his eyes.. and he sees something in mine.. but what is he trying to find.. in the mist of sitting alone in a love blind.. who is this man and what causes him to be so kind.. either a sheep in wolf's clothing, or a pearl from his designed loathing..

Is this a diamond in a rough, hmm.. maybe I should test his bluff..

So I look further into his eyes.. and to my surprise.. I don't see lies.. but I do see the silent cries.. it's no disguise of the pain in those brown eyes..

Rarity is at the core of the chip on his shoulder, more

formless as he gets older.. who is this man.. and what is his plan.. I wonder."

The crowd snaps like at a spoken word session. She smiles while putting the mic back on the stand and leaves the spotlight. Just as Seven was thinking how she had a read on him, she appears by making her way from out of the crowd. She walks pass Seven and sits at the bar where he can see her at a distance. Her intentions strikes his curiosity. He decides that he will go over and talk to her, but first make his way to the men's room to make sure he didn't have any chocolate cake in his teeth. When walking towards restrooms they both make eye contact. A neutral look of interest, followed by looking away as if it never happened.

Seven walks into the empty restroom. He starts from the first stall and begins to walk towards the last. Whichever toilet he walked passed was the cleanest is where he would enter. It happened to be the 5th stall towards the end of the restroom. He walks in and closes the stall door behind him. As he begins releasing himself, he reads the writing on the wall that was directly in front of him. It read, WHO ARE YOU? He squints at the words on the wall while zipping his zipper back up. Before flushing the toilet, the restroom door slams open by a big husky man on his cell phone.

The loud bang shook his attention. He remained still while listening to what was going on outside his stall. The man was so into his phone conversation that he forgot to see if anybody else was in the restroom with him. He paced back and forth by the sink area with anger in his voice. Before Seven was getting ready to walk out of his stall, he hears the man say, "the woman who set us up, she is up here right now. I am sure it's her, how can we forgot her?" Seven stayed put in the stall and listened to the man talk. "Yo, go start the party bus up right now and don't let anybody on. "Time for some paybacks." He ends his phone call and paused for a moment. It just hit him that someone could have been listening the whole time.

The once tense to now calm man slowly walks over to the first stall. He checks to see if anybody was inside by pushing the door wide open. Then he moves on to the second stall and looks inside. The eyes of Seven grew wide when hearing him move closer and closer. He quickly thinks of his next move. The man now moves over to the third stall to see if it was empty. He walks to the fourth stall and pushes the door open. He moves in front of the 5th stall that was closed shut and stands there. Right before he attempts to open the door, two guys come walking in the restroom talking to one another. The husky man stopped in his tracks and looks at the other two men as if everything was okay and begins to walk off. Seven let's out a big sigh of relief. He gathers himself before leaving the stall and looks back at the writing on the wall. "WHO ARE YOU?"

Seven checks himself in the mirror before walking out to join Destiny at the bar. He looks around the lounge but doesn't see her. His concern increased for the woman who grabbed his undivided attention. "It's like she knew me," he kept telling himself over and over. He pays his tab before leaving the building.

There were two parking lots, one in the front and the bigger one in the back. Seven walked towards the back of the parking lot. There was a narrow space towards the very back of the parking lot in order to exit. The exit was in between the two lane space with 2 building's standing on each side. He walked towards the narrow space that looked like a painting you could call, "a light at the end of the tunnel." While walking in the empty parking lot he notices the man standing in front of a party bus that was parked halfway to the exit. In order to make it towards that light at the end of the tunnel, he would have to pass the party bus.

Seven takes out his cell phone and pretends to be talking to someone. As he approaches closer, he can hear the voice of a woman scream from inside the bus. When walking passed the man guarding the door, he makes eye contact with Seven, "keep it moving, there just having a little fun back there. They couldn't wait until they got home." Seven nods his head up as if he understood quite clear while continuing to walk. A woman's voice screams from inside the bus once again. He could hear that a hand covered her mouth half way through shouting the words, "somebody help me!" His heart beat like a drum in his chest. His imagination came into play as he began hearing a voice on the left shoulder telling him to keep walking, while the voice on the right shoulder tells him to help her. The voices in his head convicted him more and more as he approaches closer to exiting the parking lot.

Everything is happening so fast. He asks himself the question, "how did I get myself in this situation?" The words on the wall then flashed before his eyes, "WHO ARE YOU?" He stopped walking and thought about that question. Who am I? Why am I here? He turns his head back and looks at the man who stands in front of the party bus. The big guy happened to be staring right back at him. He turns back and looks at the narrow passage way to his exit. He thinks for a moment, closes his eyes and takes a deep breath. He dials 911, as soon the operator answers is when he speaks, "there is a problem in the parking lot of the Melting Pot Lounge," and hangs up the phone. He puts his cell phone back in his pocket and turns back around towards the bus. As he approaches closer to a man guarding the bus is when he began to act lost. The big man who seemed to be a regular at the gym speaks, "just keep on moving, don't come back here." Seven ignores his request and continues to walk forward, "I'm sorry sir, I am just lost and want to know if you could help me out?"

Seven walks right up to the man and asks if he could help him before he was interrupted, "what part of don't come back here don't you understand?" Before he could finish his sentence, Seven sent a quick blow to man's Adam's apple. He immediately clutches his throat and stumbles to one knee while grasping for air. Seven then walks up a couple steps to the party bus door. He walks in chanting, "heyyy, party over here," while waving his hands in the air. The whole inside was lit up neon blue. While putting on an act, he sees a man forcing himself to sexually penetrate the very woman from inside the lounge. Her strength was just about all drained from putting up a fight. Her nose was bleeding and parts of her clothes had been ripped off. The abuser quickly pulled up his pants and turned back at Seven, "who the hell are you?" Seven was moving in closer while still waving his hands in the air, "party over here!" Once Seven stepped closer at a good distance, he hit the man in the jaw with a swift right hook that came down from being waved in the air. His right hook drops the man on to the seat next to a battered Destiny. She gave a look of relief once realizing someone came to her rescue. She stretches her hand out towards Seven.

DESTINY: Please help me.

SEVEN: (Taking her hand and picking her up) I got you.

DESTINY: (With her head on the shoulder of Seven and her mouth near his ear) You saved me.

SEVEN: You are going to be okay.

Seven lifts Destiny up in his arms and carries her to the front of the bus. Right when he opened the door, the barrow of a gun was pointed right between his eyes. The big man guided Seven where to go with his pistol with one hand and clutched his neck with the other. Seven steps down from the bus while the tip of the gun was aimed steady at his head. He orders Seven to put the woman down. He did not want to lay her on the concrete ground so he laid her on the hood of the nearest parked car. It just so happened to be a shiny red old school Ford mustang. Soon as he laid her in the most comfortable position, he received a blow from the back of head that dropped him to the ground.

While lying on the ground, Seven could see the man he punched inside the party bus run out towards the action. Kicks to the ribs and punches to the head is what Seven could feel. Both men beat the living daylight out of Seven. From an aerial view looking down from the sky, you would see a beautiful Destiny laying faced up on the hood of a red Ford car and Seven being kicked and punched by two men. Her eyes stare at the dark sky while Seven becomes a sacrificial lamb. "Get the girl, bring her with us," the man shouts after kicking the unconscious Seven. He grabs her arm and pulls her off the car. He drags her towards the bus just as there were more people in the parking lot running up to see the chaos. Police sirens were approaching fast.

The combination of hearing the police sirens and more witnesses, the man releases Destiny's hand and the two ran into the party bus and took off. Destiny picks herself off the ground and slowly walks over to the unconscious Seven. Police sirens from afar were approaching closer. Destiny stands over Seven while wiping blood from her nose and fixing her clothes. A stranger from a parking lot asks if she was okay. She gets on her knees and leans down to see if Seven was still breathing. She then embraced Seven and kissed him on his cheek.

There was a loud honk from a car at the end of the parking lot. Destiny looks to identify the car in the narrow space in between the two buildings. Once she could see that it was a black Cadillac she spoke the word, "King." Police sirens were becoming louder. The red and blue police lights were coming from the front parking lot of the building. Destiny starts walking towards the black Cadillac. Once the driver of the Cadillac sees the red and blue police lights, he turns into the parking lot and drives towards Destiny. He swings the car with the passenger door open to where she could hop right in and no one would be able to read the license plate. He drives off in a cloudy smoke right as the police drove up to the scene. By the time the white smoke cleared, the Cadillac was out of sight. The driver was the older brother of Destiny named, King.

DESTINY: Brother.

KING: Are you okay! Are you hurt?

DESTINY: No, I'll be fine, just a little sore.

KING: What's the deal Destiny! You wasn't going to tell me until you were in trouble?

DESTINY: I'm sorry, I didn't know I would run into to any trouble.

KING: That was a close call. Are you trying to blow everything! Huh?

DESTINY: I know big bro, it won't happen again.

KING: We almost there Destiny! We gotta stay focused!

DESTINY: I am focused King, I was out seeing if I could reel one in.

KING: You know the rules! What would have happen if I would have lost you tonight! Then what? You know its people out here looking for us.

DESTINY: It won't happen again.

KING: We gotta make sure that there will be a next time.

DESTINY: I know, I get it!

KING: (Calming down while pulling up to a stop light) Look I'm sorry for yelling, that was just too close. I can't lose you, you're all I got out here in this world. And I damn sure ain't going back to prison. Look at me sister, who did this to you? What happen?

Destiny looks up at her handsome dark skin brother with his bottom teeth were shinning gold inside the dark shaded Cadillac. His bone structure tightened from trying to hold in his anger while waiting for her response.

DESTINY: It was one of the Northside boys who we hit over a year ago. The one bad move that caused us to never shit to close to home again. I admit.. I wasn't out trying to reel anybody in. I was just at home bored and wanted to go out on my own. No disguise, no intentions or motives. I need that sometimes King. As a woman I have certain needs and you have to understand that.

KING: (While driving he looks Destiny in the eyes

without saying a word)

DESTINY: I was at this place tonight because I wanted to be regular for once. And maybe just have a genuine conversation with a man. And before that was going to happen, I was spotted by one of the Northside boys. I tried to leave but they had me trapped in. One stood by the exit door to meet me. They brought me to this party bus. He was saying how we were going to pay back everything we took, or he was going to kill me. He repeatedly asked me where you were. And since I didn't tell him he began to slap me around. That's when he started ripping my clothes off. I tried to fight him but he was to strong.

KING: Did he rape you?

DESTINY: (Pause with no answer while wiping away tears)

King: Did he rape you!

DESTINY: No. He almost did.. but right before he was about to force himself in me, a man came in the bus and prevented the man from raping me. Once he tried to take me away, they jumped him. They beat him bad. Oh Lord please don't let him die.

KING: The man, who was this man that helped you?

Destiny then pulled out the wallet and keys of Seven. She opens his wallet and says his name, "Seven."

KING: (Taking the drivers license from her hand and holding it up to where he could see for himself) Seven.

The number of completion.. How did you get his wallet and keys?

DESTINY: When he was laid out on the ground unconscious. There were people in the parking lot watching, so when I gave him a hug is when I picked pocket him.

Chapter 3

APARTMENT# 2111

THE NEXT MORNING

K ing sat inside a four door Honda while smoking his black & mild cigar. He blew the smoke towards the driver's license held out in his hand. He ponders the thought, "what causes a man to do such a courageous act for a stranger?" He wastes no more time and begins typing the address into the GPS system. Once the address pops up, he realizes that Seven lives in the inner city projects. He checks to make sure his insurance card, tags, blinkers and brake lights were all in good standards to avoid any reason to be stopped by the police. He sits up straight and puts his seatbelt on before driving off. The directions led King to the actual complex building where Seven lives. He googles the closest hospital to the Melting Pot night club. Once he finds the phone number he makes the call.

REPRESENTATIVE: This is the Legacy Health Center, my name is Shirl Williams, how may I help you?

KING: Good morning, I am trying to see if my brother was rushed to this hospital last night.

REPRESENTATIVE: What's the name?

KING: His name is Seven Fitzgerald.

REPRESENTATIVE: Hold please.

KING: Yes ma'am (he holds for a brief moment while watching a drug addict walk by the car)

REPRESENTATIVE: Yes, Seven Fitzgerald is here. He is located in ICU on the 3rd floor in room #333.

KING: I thank you for your help Miss Williams.

The information was stored in the memory bank. He gets out of the car he uses as his disguise. His demanding presence caused enough attention as it is. King stood six foot three inches tall. Slim but firm. He was shaped like an in shape boxer. He had dark skin, wore a gold grill on his 6 bottom teeth, had a bald fade haircut with a three inch part right in the middle of his hair line. He had a presence of a lion and the poise of a eagle.

King walks closer to the vicinity of Seven's apartment. He removes his keys out of his pocket when moving up to the second floor. He walks without the look of suspicion, although his awareness covers all parameters. He steps in front of apartment #2111 and begins to knock on the door. No answer. He waits for a moment and knocks again. He looks around to see if anybody was watching him before opening the door from the outside. He enters and shuts the door behind him. "Maintenance, here to fix the toilet." No answer from anybody inside so the coast was clear. He takes a stroll around the small efficiency apartment. The first thing he notices is the big window in the small apartment.

King walks over and takes a peep out the window that allows you to see a large amount of the apartment complex. Kids were playing amongst themselves, while people hung outside of their front door. One group of adults played dominoes while a few youngster's played basketball. On the desk next to the window, there were several writings on white sheets of paper. A few books were stacked near a laptop computer. He opened a few drawers to find a buried bachelor's degree at the bottom. A man with a bachelor's degree in Sociology living in a small efficiency apartment seemed a little odd to King.

Vinyl's were stacked along the wall on one side of the apartment. There was DJ equipment, turn tables and a microphone. A record player rested on a stand near a guitar. King stood there a while mentally picking the brain of the absent Seven. "A music lover indeed," he speaks to himself while walking towards the kitchen. He looks in the refrigerator to only see bottled waters, fruits, and vegetables. He looks inside the pantry to only see there being enough food to last a few days. There was peanut butter, jelly, oatmeal, bags of beans and several bottles of natural herbs. He picks a couple of bottles up and glances at the nutrition facts. He walks over to the closet and looks inside. Not very many clothes and shoes for Seven, although the clothes he did have were fairly nice. There was at least two sets for every occasion. King checks the labels of the clothes and notices that none of them were named brand.

Suspicion and curiosity were in the eyes of the intrigued King. He found the man who saved his sister to be an interesting one. A simple man who happens to be a lover of the artistry field of writing and music. There were many books but no television inside the small efficiency apartment. The healthy choice of food and natural herbs led him to believe that Seven used his body as a temple. His clothes were not named brand which led him to believe that Seven was not caught up in labels or status. Or, he did not live above his means.

King walks over to the record player and drops the needle on the vinyl. The vintage scratching noise that a record makes begins as he walks over and looks out the window. As soon as the song began to play, all of King's movements stopped. He looks back at the record player and squints his eyes. The Marvin Gaye album, "What's Going On," plays throughout the room. The song hit King so hard to where he sat down on the chair in front of Seven's desk. Tears ran down the straight face of King. It took him back to a place in his life where everything changed. "Who was this man Seven," he thought to himself.

 King walked over to the vinyl's that were faced up. To his amazement, every artist he witnessed just happened to be one of his favorites. Marvin Gaye, Bob Dylan, Miles Davis, John Coltrane and Erykah Badu to name a few. His curiosity for Seven grew on him by the moment. King switched the vinyl record once he ran across one of his all time favorite albums by Miles Davis, "Kind of Blue." He sits at the desk while staring into space. The laid back jazz of Miles Davis played throughout the room while King picks up a piece of paper and begins to read the writing...

"At home performing the art of being alone.. Silent is the mode on my phone as my mind roams though like a flying drone of the things God has shown. I'm focused, often feed the homeless.. faith filled, no hocus pocus, nor bogus lies to get self noticed. It's just when love isn't enough, and your not moved by stuff.. getting to know self was a must. That's when I quenched my thirst, in understanding my worth here on earth. I can remember there being love and music ever since birth.. Cool vibes when I arrive from being alive.. 360 waves on bee hive, take a dive into my mental hard drive, flip through the archive.. I'm prepared to help revive the deprived. I crawled out of pits from hitting rock bottom.. A solver of problems who can teach to defeat the goblins.. To stay strong in this game although hurt and hobbling. I can feel an attack of the spiritual beast come before it's released from its leash. From a mess into a message, blessed to be a blessing."

King stops reading from being impressed. The poetry went right along with the jazz in the background. He could feel the poetry, the word play and arrangement of words that pieced together so well. King connected with the writing so much that he thought it was something he would have wrote himself. He felt anything that was real and honest. He then put the piece of paper down and picked up another one with writings on it. He began to read while the jazz of Miles Davis continued to play.

"You see, the enemy doesn't want us to believe, so therefore the spirit of the unseen beast sends it's G's in the form of joy snatching thieves, the cause of disease, corrupt decision makers who deceive due to greed.. False prophets speak of hidden agenda's to gain profit, but I'm plugged into the source so I don't entertain their socket. I mentally block it, do my research, ask to be led, then take off like a rocket.. Cool, calm and collective like Tom Brady in the pocket.."

King puts the paper down while in deep thought. He looks around the small apartment while puzzling all the pieces to the puzzle together. He stands and stares out the window while sporadically looking back down at the writings on the piece of paper. "Who is this man and why am I here," he thought to himself. He then reached in his pocket and took out his cell phone. He called his sister Destiny.

DESTINY: What's the word?

KING: I'm over at his apartment.

DESTINY: So what are you thinking?

KING: What do you remember about this man?

DESTINY: It was brief, but in that small amount of time, I felt something genuine. I felt something real.

KING: Is that so...... after scoping his place out, I feel the same way.

DESTINY: Is that Miles Davis I hear in the background?

KING: It is indeed.

DESTINY: Speaks volumes.

KING: When you looked into his eyes, what did you see?

DESTINY: I saw a strong, wise, broken man who was set apart from this world.

KING: What makes you think he is set apart?

DESTINY: He was alone on his birthday. He mentioned how he doesn't drink but he decided to drink that night. I was thinking to myself, what's a courteous, handsome and humble man doing out by himself.

KING: I've never heard you speak of a man like this.

DESTINY: He read my move by spotting out my

intention. No man has ever read me like that besides you.

KING: And this very man we speak of, saved my sister from being raped huh (a moment of silence).

DESTINY: Not only did he save me, those men were determined to find you by any means.

KING: Looks like we found something here.

DESTINY: Is he still alive is the question though?

KING: Yes he is, I called the hospital and he is there. I'm about to go pay him a visit. I'll call you soon.

DESTINY: Ok, I love you.

KING: I love you to sister.

King notices some opened mail in the trash can next to the desk. Bills, a returned letter from a people search company and a letter from the leasing office threatening to evict him. King hears some children playing outside that blends in with the jazz. His mind in deep thought while he picks up the chrome ink pen that Seven writes with. He wonders if he were to ever write a book and how would it be perceived. It was hard for him to believe that the story of his life was duplicated. The opposite attracted the slim basketball built man who mentally broke down Seven. King was not one who trusted many, but he felt a connection with Seven although they have never met. The no television, the cleanness of his home, the music, books and paper with writing's on it. It reminded him sitting in his cell while in prison.

King leaves the apartment and locks the door behind him. He walks downstairs and goes in whatever direction he feels the leasing office would be. He walked passed a woman who was a prostitute, "hey sexy, where you going," in a flirtatious demeanor. She looked way older than her age. "Thank you babe, I'm looking for the leasing office. Can you point me in the right direction?" While pointing in the direction, "yea it's on Knox street." while digging in his pocket and pulling out some money, "thank you momma, here you go.""Ewww won't he do it, won't he do it!" My prayer was answered this morning, thank ya Jesus!" King looks at the total appreciation on her face for receiving a twenty dollar bill. "Thank you," and begins walking in the direction of Knox Street. He walks into the leasing office and sits in the chair right in front of the worker, Mr. Jones who was on the phone.

Mr. JONES: I have been working with you Miss. Yalonda. Now, I don't want to evict ya, but I need to see some money in front of me by.. uhh, let me see, uhh.. last week! Now I ain't tryna get in ya pocket book or coin purse, but I know you ain't broke like your saying. I see the pizza man knocking on your door, and a couple of ya kid's wearing Air Jordan shoes. Babe you on the government assistant programs of all the program's, hell, ya rent ain't nothing, $120 dollar's. I'll be right with you sir.

KING: No worries.

Mr. JONES: I know the game, don't you play me Miss Yalonda. I don't want to hear it, because I done heard it all! Now, you know I ain't gonna have you and those poor babies out on the curb, but you better not be trying to play me. Find a way to get me my money. And the next time you find yourself raising your voice at me, there will be an eviction notice for ya ass real quick and fast. Don't play me young lady. Have a good day... What can I do for you sir?

KING: Yes, my name is KJ, I am a friend of Seven Fitzgerald in apartment #2111.

Mr. JONES: Oh yea, there is another one who owes me money. That half breed been ducking and dodging me the last few days.

KING: He hasn't been dodging you. He has been in the hospital from an accident that occurred.

Mr. JONES: Well alright, thanks for letting me know, but that don't pay the rent. When he is supposed to be getting out of the hospital?

KING: In about a week, may even two weeks.

Mr. JONES: Aw hell naw! He running game. He got the wrong one jack. Now I pray for the man, but he will need more prayer's, because there will be an eviction notice on his door.

KING: Well that's what brings me to you. I am here to relay a message from Seven. He tells me to tell you, that he is sorry for being late with his response. He wasn't trying to avoid you. So I am going to give KJ the money to pay my rent. I am KJ.

Mr. JONES: Well, we have rules and regulations. And no one is above is law. I would need a signed money order or check from Seven. Then, I won't draw up the eviction notice for his late yella ass. I'm tired of this shit.

KING: How about we get right to it, while I'm sitting right here. The main thing is, you receiving the money. Mr. Seven is in hospital as we speak for performing a heroic act. And with all due respect sir, let that be the last time you speak negatively on my friend Seven. Do we have an understanding on that?

Mr. JONES (Long pause, with a look of who does this guy think he is) Excuse me! Who do you think you are by coming in my office, telling me what I ain't gon do?

KING: (Staring in the eyes of Mr. Jones while not speaking)

Mr. JONES: Uh hello. And besides, you can't just walk up in here and pay, how you want to pay? So we will handle this the right way. The same way of how I been running it. Now, do we have an understanding on that?

King slowly gets up from his chair. He lifts the chair up a few inches from the ground, while walking around the desk towards Mr. Jones. The older man slightly tilted his head down while watching King over the top bridge of his thick glasses, "sir what are doing," in a nervous tone. King replies while telling him everything was going to be okay, he was just hard on hearing and needed to sit a little closer. King pulls the chair right next to Mr. Jones and sits down while never taking his eyes off his eyes. He leans forward a little closer to Mr. Jones.

KING: I respect all my elder's. But I also don't like to repeat myself or being talked to in a disrespectful manner. So I am going tell you one more time, up close and personal so you can feel my energy. Now, it would be a very wise time to lose the pride and hear me out because that pride will getcha every time. And after you hear me out, we can both win. Now, this is what is going to happen. I am going to pay you Seven's rent and I am also going to pay the rent of the following month as well. The woman you were on the phone with, Miss Yolanda, I am going to pay her rent for this last month and this month and I am going to pay it all in cash. And you are going to excuse the money order thing this time and you are going to figure it out. And for the late fees and for your troubles, I am also going to give you enough money to do something nice for yourself. Or if you are married, you can take your wife to the nicest restaurant in town. Now, do we have an understanding on that?

Mr. JONES: (Total change in his demeanor) Oh we most certainly do. What did you say your name is again?

KING: KJ

Mr. JONES: Right on KJ. So you say you will be paying

in cash, is that correct?

KING: That is correct sir. I'm glad we could come to an understanding on this matter. I'm sure you have been working hard and it's time to treat yourself.

Mr. JONES. Bingo! You are spot on my man.

KING: (While counting money) I will definitely take care of that for you.

Mr. JONES: Show ya right. Is there anything else I can do for you Mr. KJ?

KING: (While handing Mr. Jones the money) You know, I'm glad you asked, because there is something you can do for me.

Mr. JONES: Shoot

KING: (While handing Mr. Jones an extra $100) Can you keep a close look out for his apartment #2111. Just for the next couple of weeks, no cleaning people, no pest control, no random pop ups at this location. Nobody needs to enter this location. Seven, he is going to need to be on some total peace, total bed rest type of thing until he gets well.

Mr. JONES: Well I'll be.. (While looking at the extra $100 bill over the top bridge of his glasses). That's a done deal partner.

 KING: Pleasure doing business with you.

Mr. JONES: And the same to you. Man o man, I have

been around them all and you are one smooth criminal. Well, maybe not the criminal part, but you know what I mean.

King doesn't respond back but mentally thinks about what Mr. Jones said. He places the chair back in its correct place, checks the time on his gold watch and leaves the office. He walks to his car and leaves in the direction of the Legacy Hospital. The soundtrack to the movie, The Godfather plays while making calculative chess moves in his mind. Once King has his mind set on a task, it becomes his life. The project stays on his mind until the task is complete. He mentally goes through all the pro's and con's. Every detail of options are thought out and not attempted until it's all mentally played out with precise precision. He will eat, sleep, and breath the task with the aim to have everything go as planned. King was a perfectionist, while it's safe to say, that he was bit of a germophobic. He had to have things clean, in order, and prepared. The saying fits best when it came to King, "never judge a book by its cover," because he most definitely did not fit the perception of his outer appearance.

King arrives at the hospital and makes his way to the third floor. He walks to the front desk and speaks to the first nurse he sees. He gives Seven's wallet and keys to the receptionist while briefly stating that he retrieved the items after Seven was rushed to the hospital. He portrays to be the brother of Seven to get more information on his health and to see if he has had any visitors since his arrival. He walks over to room #333 and enters the room. Before walking over to the bed side, he stands there at a distance and looks at him sleep. He walks over and watches the man who sparred his life a world of trouble. He then walks over to the window and sits in the chair that faces Seven. For the next three hours, King sat and watched the parking lot without barely moving.

Then finally, Seven awakes to first see the ceiling. He continues to look up while collecting his thoughts of where he was at and how he got there. When turning to the side, he sees a stranger sitting in a chair staring right at him. The way he was sitting could have been a portrait painting. King rested both elbows on the arm of the chair with his hands folded on his stomach. He was sitting with his long legs crossed. He looked like a classy sophisticated man who was raised by the street's his whole life. He wore a cool top and bottom jump suit that matched his shoes. His bottom gold teeth matched his gold watch. He had a razor sharp edge up and clean cut face. Seven and King saw each other for the first time.

KING: And so he awakes.

SEVEN: Who are you? Look man I didn't know that woman, I was just trying to help. Nurse!

KING: No need for that Seven.

SEVEN: How do you know my name? Nurse!

KING: I overheard the nurse when asking about your state of being.

• • •

SEVEN: (Showing signs of having a sore body and headache) Look man, I don't know anything. Everything happened so fast. When I think about it, things just got crazy after I made a wish and blew out the candle.

KING: So do you believe in fate?

SEVEN: (Thinks before he speaks) Yea I believe in fate.

KING: Then what are you worried about? Then it is possible that after you made a wish, right after you went through the sacrifice that leads you closer to fulfilling that wish.

SEVEN: You could be the man sent by the two guys who jumped me for all I know. The man standing in the way of me fulfilling my Destiny.

KING: I could be, but then again, maybe not. Call off the nurse when she comes so we can talk.

SEVEN: Who are you?

KING: (Gets up and walks to the edge of the hospital bed) I am King. And I came here to thank you.

The Nurse: (Walks into the room) "Oh you are finally up. Are you okay?"

SEVEN: (While staring back at King) Yes I'm okay. Do I have any major damage? And what is in this cord I'm hooked up to?

The Nurse: No major damage, but you did suffer from

a concussion. Your body just needs rest from being banged up pretty bad. We gave you an IV to avoid dehydration.

SEVEN: Thank you. Can you please give us a minute?

The Nurse: (While looking at King but talking to Seven) Are you sure everything is okay? Is this man your brother? He says that you two were brothers. Do you need me to call security?

KING: Yes that is so, we are brothers. And we have a sister by the name of, Destiny June.

King could see that Destiny's name got his attention. He then informs the nurse that everything is okay and she then leaves out of the room.

KING: I truly thank you for helping my sister Destiny. She is all that I got. And I am here to talk business with you. I would like to show my appreciation. And by the way, Destiny would like to see you.

SEVEN: She is a very interesting woman.

KING: She is indeed. You haven't even seen the half of it.

SEVEN: So what business do you speak of? And you don't owe me anything.

KING: Oh but I do. A business move that will benefit us both.

SEVEN: I don't like doing business with strangers. And

I have a hard time trusting.

KING: I second that. But you do believe in fate. So what do you have to lose?

SEVEN: Alright, I'm listening.

KING: I say we leave and talk elsewhere, the men who jumped you can show up any minute. That's why I was here, just in case they decided to show up.

SEVEN: (Shakes his head in disappointment) Look, your welcome for me helping your sister. I just happened to be there, anybody could have been in my shoes and did the same thing. It's probably just best if you leave.

KING: I respect that. But to answer your question of, why? It means a lot to me because that woman you saved from a man almost raping her, happens to be a virgin. I raised her. Not to mention, they could have killed her to find me. And it would be an honor if I could show my appreciation.

Seven pulls off the cord that is attached to him and slowly lifts himself up from the bed. He puts both feet on the ground and stands up. He walks over to window and begins to stare outside while taking in what King just informed him.

SEVEN: (While looking out the window) You can look out a window and see a picture in motion worth a thousand words. This life. This world we live in. A virgin in this modern world. What a rare case she is.

KING: How about we go get something to eat. I will tell you what caused you to end up in this hospital. The reason behind it all. And later we will meet up with Destiny for dinner. At least allow us to show our respect for what you have done for us. Then you can be on your way. You have to understand, you are like a hero to us.

SEVEN: (Eyes grew wide open while looking out the window) Say, there's one of the guys who jumped me last night!

KING: (Walks over to the window to see for himself) We have to go now. You are going to have to trust me or deal with these men coming to look for you.

They both hurry out of the room. Seven left out wearing his hospital gown. He didn't bother to retrieve any of his possessions. Instead, he asked a nurse where the stairs where located. "I'm sorry sir, the stair case is under construction right now and off limits."

SEVEN: You gotta be kidding me, of all the times in the world.

KING: The elevator is our only option.

SEVEN: That guy is probably on his way up right now.

KING: (While looking up to see if there were any surveillance cameras near the elevator's) If we run into him I'll have to take him out. I'm not in the mood to run and I don't think you are in the condition to run as well.

Both men walk to the elevator area. They watch to see who will be coming out of the opening doors. There were elevators on both sides of the hall. A nurse come out from the reception desk and watched the two men leave, "sir you shouldn't be getting out of bed." Seven and King pay her no mind as King pushes the first floor bottom to the elevators. The nurse still talks from at a distance causing an unwanted scene of people to see what was going on. Both Seven and King stood facing the elevator door that made the noise to notify the door was about to open. The elevator door had a mirror reflection. The two stood impatiently but patiently waiting for the door to open. They both looked into the mirror that displayed what was happening behind them. Not only could the man come out from behind them, but the door in front of them as well. A moment right before they knew the door was about to open, King grips his fist ready for action.

Finally, the door slides open and a couple of people walk out. The big boy from the Northside not being one of them. They walk into the elevator and King pushes the first floor bottom that lights up. As the elevator door remains open, you could see the elevator door on the other side opening up and people walk out. The Northside guy did not see King or Seven when walking out, although both King and Seven could see him. The husky man would have continued on walking but the nurse who caused a scene was still trying to get Seven's attention. That caused the big man who stood in the middle of the elevators to pay attention to what she was saying. "Stop those two gentlemen who just got onto the elevator." The man turned his head and looked inside the elevators to see both King and Seven standing there while looking right back at him. He then raced for the elevator door but it closed just in the nic of time.

SEVEN: Yo! Who are these people?

KING: Some boys from the Northside who are looking for revenge.

SEVEN: Man let's get the hell away from here.

KING: Roger that. No worries.

The elevator door opens and they both run to the parking lot. The hospital gown flapped in the air while following King's lead to the car. Seven forgot all about his headache from the adrenaline rush of trying get away. They both got inside the car and King pulls out from the parking spot. When making a left turn into the main entrance, they could see the Northside guy run out from the hospital. He spots out King and Seven inside the Honda. They have to drive passed him in order to leave the parking lot. They all made eye contact before King hits the gas and drives straight for the man standing in the middle of the street. The big man attempts to stand in front of the car but realizes that King didn't have any plans on stopping. The big man dashes out of the way and King drives away. Seven watches the big man from the rear view mirror as they drive off.

SEVEN: That was close.

KING: (Smiling while looking at Seven) Yea it was.

SEVEN: Is this funny to you, do you get a thrill out of this?

KING: Naw, but it was fun though. A new story to tell your kids one day.

SEVEN: Yea, if we make it to see the day.

KING: Mattew 8: 26, and he saith unto them, why are ye fearful, O ye of little faith? Then he arose, and rebuked the winds and the sea; and there was a great calm.

SEVEN: Interesting.

KING: Fate is interesting indeed.

SEVEN: Who are you?

KING: That's a good question. But the real question is, who are you? I sense that you are hungry. How about some brunch? Then I will answer your question

Chapter

4

I AM KING

KING: (Driving) How are you feeling over there champ?

SEVEN: (Rubbing the side of his rib cage) Yea, I'll be cool, but I'll be cooler when this headache goes away.

KING: I know this ducked-off dinner that has a variety of food. Get some good food in you and you will feel stronger. I know the feeling.

SEVEN: Wait man. I thank you but, maybe it's just best if you dropped me off at home. No offense but I don't know you.

KING: I could definitely do that. But, before I make a U turn, allow me to remind you, that man who we just dodged is looking for you, in order to find to me. These

• • •

guys are ruthless, they seek to destroy. There is a possibility that he will find out your name and have his people locate where you live. If you are not prepared to have a strong duck and dodge game, then it's best if you hear me out. Even if you don't have any information to give to them, they will still beat you unconscious. Or even possibly kill you for causing Destiny to get away.

SEVEN: One day you are chillin, minding your own business and just like that, you are being hunted.

KING: Cold world ain't it.

SEVEN: Yea, cold world is right. And I like staying warm, that's why I stay out of the way.

KING: What if it's not in your purpose to stay out of the way?

SEVEN: I've thought about that very question for many days and nights. And I don't know the answer to that.

KING: Your answer will come.

SEVEN: Why are these people after you and Destiny?

KING: If it's not too much to ask, I would rather tell you while we sit down. I think I'll have me some coffee. I did sit up and stare outside the window for a few hours while you laid in that hospital bed. I haven't shared with anybody who I really am, so it's taking me a while. But now is the time.

SEVEN: That's understood. I know without knowing, the movie to your life doesn't go straight to DVD, it goes straight to the theater.

KING: An entertaining one, hopefully it doesn't end as I vision it. Thought's, sometimes you can't control them. Anyways, let's go eat.

SEVEN: I'd like to put some clothes on but I'm starving. I don't even know where my wallet and keys are.

KING: Don't worry about a thing, I'll make sure you have whatever you need. I don't think it's a good idea to go back to your apartment today. Better safe than sorry.

SEVEN: Right, I think I'll pass on getting beat up, I want to go in the opposite direction of that.

KING: I hear ya.. but in the meantime, I got my mind set on a plate of steak and eggs. Maybe some grits and hash browns on the side.

The two men walked inside the dinner and sat in a booth by the window. They both order their food without looking at the menu. King put the cream and sugar in his coffee while Seven squeezed the lemon juice in the water.

KING: Destiny and I are like the modern day Bonnie and Clyde, but only she is my sister. But we don't rob just anybody. We rob the bad guys. The ones who aren't making the world a better place and needs to be taught a lesson. Could be someone who's ego needs to be humbled. A drug dealer who likes to sell to the youth or a pregnant woman. You know, things of that nature.

And these gentlemen are more than likely to be rolling in some cash. This is where Destiny comes in. Cat woman or Super woman don't have shit on her. She is one cold blooded woman.

SEVEN: Who happens to be a virgin, and does poetry off the top of her head.

KING: That's right. I'm like her father. Besides the four years I spent in prison, I have been in her life. She earned her bachelor's degree in those four years. Which can be helpful, but mainly used for resources and disguise. Being in disguise is her expertise. She can play the role of different characters to draw in these particular group of men. She draws them in, then I become their karma. I don't harm them if they cooperate. I don't break their bank, but I definitely put a dent in that bitch.

These two men who jumped you, we robbed them awhile back. And we hittem for a pretty penny. That was the one mistake. Those guys have a big name out here and it was to close to home. That's when we started traveling from city to city, going on hitting sprees. Rack up enough money to last us some seasons. When we start to get low, we plan, prepare and execute. We been hustling since we were kids. Just so we can eat. We rarely slip up, but this one time we did and now these people are after us. Destiny went out and just happened to be seen that night at the Melting Pot Club. And that's when you came in the picture. I don't think you understand how it would have destroyed me if Destiny would have been raped. Especially with her being a virgin. That really means a lot to her and myself. She is the only thing I am proud of.

SEVEN: (Looking around to see if there are any movie camera's around watching them) Are we in a movie right now? That is one interesting story, until I came into the picture. Is this even real? Am I still knocked unconscious and this is all a dream?

KING: (Gold teeth shining from smiling) No dream, this is all real.

SEVEN: Are you on the run?

KING: Naw, I'm more like a ghost. Until last night, we finally got problems. But what the problem doesn't realize is, I am the problem when you mess with my people. Over time I learned to play chess and keep my ego under control. I could easily go looking for them but that could start a war. With it being so close to home, I must play chess. Be smarter and wiser.

SEVEN: So what's the next play?

KING: I'm thinking those guys could be looking for us, so maybe it's time to go on a work vacation. Think and plan out the next move while relaxing in a nice hotel and eating like a boss.

SEVEN: Well I must say, that is one of the most interesting stories I've heard in all of my life. So what do you do it for?

KING: One of the main goals is to retire at a young age and have a family. And for Destiny to live the life she desires. It's very difficult to have the life we desire by living the way it is designed. It's designed for us to be workers. Modern day slaves to run somebody elses business. It's not in me to live that kind of life. I don't want to answer to nobody, or be controlled by man. Man is evil. Man can be selfish. Including myself. Even if I want to go out and get a good paying job, who out here is going to hire a convicted felon with this black skin and gold teeth. But you know how that goes. I could go on and on about this system being ran out here.

SEVEN: I understand. I'm on the same page.

KING: I get it how I get it. I'm not proud of what I do, but not having to make pennies at a 9 to 5 from using my mind helps me sleep better at night. One weekend might bring enough to hold us over for half a year.

The waitress arrives with their food. The jelly was spread out on the toast, salt and pepper shaked on the eggs, ketchup on the hash browns and a steak being cut with a knife and fork, while they both continue conversing.

SEVEN: Must be nice to sit back in financial comfort for a weekend's worth of work.

KING: It's not worth it. I'm ready to be retired already and run me a business. As you see, karma will eventually come to collect. Now someone is looking for me. A mission could go bad and somebody I rob might decide not lay down so easy. They might go for broke and be willing to die for theirs. If we don't play our cards right, we could lose our lives. Not to mention the thing that I am not proud of, it all takes its toll on you.

SEVEN: The pros and cons to it all. Do you think it's all worth it?

KING: I believe so. I really don't know what being happy feels like. I just live and go to my strengths. Do what I know to do. I know one thing, being chewed out by someone who is nowhere near my pedigree and sitting in traffic for two hours ain't happening, no sir.

SEVEN: I've been there before, wasn't for me I must admit, your story moves me. I'm not easily moved.

KING: That Honda we drove in, it's just a disguise car. I'm getting burned out though. Ready to be legit. Robbing folks is the main source of how I make money. To have money consistently coming in, I sell drugs to two clients who I believe will not run their mouths. Far as they are concerned, I'm a ghost.

SEVEN: Why only two clients?

KING: I find less to be best. Less people you deal with, the less drama. It's powder crack cocaine, so the money comes. I won't sell to nobody but them. I don't want any traffic. These two people I would let in my home. They take care of themselves and earn their own money, it just that bad habit. Addicts are not to be trusted, but what I learned over time is that, if you look out for them, protect them, have the fix they need, and have instilled fear in them, they will be loyal to you. Sometimes even more than a close friend. But at the end of the day, there is a price to pay for everything that we do. I do dirt to make my money, while taking the wisest route possible to stay out of the cage.

SEVEN: Your one fearless man with a plan. Hearing all of this inspires me to write.

KING: So we have a writer on our hands.

SEVEN: Not really, but something like that.

KING: What do you write about?

SEVEN: Whatever comes to mind. From short stories, poetry, to songs, really anything.

KING: So when is your book coming out?

SEVEN: Ha, I don't know man. I should have an answer for you but I don't. I'm working on this thing. I really don't know why, but something is just telling me to write it. If I had an idea that was as interesting as your life story, I'd write something like that.

KING: So is that why we crossed paths?

SEVEN: What is that?

KING: Maybe it's meant for you to come with Destiny and I on a work vacation. And on this vacation, I talk and while you listen, record or write, or all three. I could give plenty of stories to go along with your own imagination. When you are not writing in your luxurious hotel room, you can be out enjoying yourself. A getaway where you can shop, eat, drink, and be merry.

SEVEN: I've been hearing that eat, drink, and be merry lately.

KING: Maybe it's time to live. Have you been living?

SEVEN: That actually sounds pretty good. But I couldn't go on a lavish robbery spree with you. I don't want to speak it into existence but, there is a possibility you could get caught.

KING: Not if I tell the cops we held you against your own will. Not if we admit that you had nothing to do with it. Not if they look in my cell phone and see that Destiny and I had a discussion of capturing you.

SEVEN: (Smiling) Your good.

KING: Besides, you could be laid up in your hotel room or out spending money somewhere on the town. Destiny and I will do our thing. Or, you could even witness us in live action. Mess around and have you a number one best seller.

SEVEN: I love the sound of that, number one best seller.

KING: Yea, now were talking.

SEVEN: It seems like you already had this planned. I mean, soon as I told you I write, you came up with an idea just like that. An idea that I would actually enjoy writing.

KING: Look man. You just saved my sister. And it's not wise for you to be at your home for a few days. After performing such a heroic act, it's time to celebrate. It's time to feel appreciated. It's time to be rewarded. So why not go and kick your feet up? It doesn't have to be a work vacation for you. You can do nothing but ask questions and take it all in, and when we get back, you can write whatever you like. Just don't use our names of course. So don't worry about money. As matter of fact, when is the last time you have been on a vacation?

SEVEN: (Starts to look out the diner window while finishing his last bite to eat) I couldn't even tell you. Maybe since I was a teenager.

KING: And why is that?

SEVEN: I've always wanted to travel, just never got around to it I guess. Maybe I just haven't been living. This plan sounds great but I'm not prepared. I would at least need to go home and pack.

KING: No need to go back to your place. We can go get everything you need right now. Underwear, socks, toiletries, and a couple of outfits to wear for now. Soon as we get into the new city we will go shop for new clothes and shoes, and whatever else you need far as cologne, a nice watch or shades.

SEVEN: (Massages his head with a confused look) Am I still knocked unconscious? There is a lot going on in my head. So many thoughts. Some big football looking dude could be sitting outside my front door waiting on me to get home.

KING: (Signals for the waitress to come over) Well, while you think about it I'll pay for the tab.

WAITRESS: You ready for the check?

KING: Yes ma'am.

SEVEN: I'm going to hit this restroom up.

KING: I'll be in the car.

Seven walks to the men's room and lands at the first urinal stall. While releasing himself, he closed his eyes and prayed silently. Asking God to guide his steps and protect him along the way. He ends his prayer once hearing someone walk in the restroom. The first thing the man sees walking in is Seven standing there peeing with a hospital gown on and his eyes closed while looking up to the ceiling. The man goes to the furthest urinal away from Seven with a, "what did I just see face," on the way there. Seven looks in the mirror while washing his hands wondering how his life just took a big turn of events.

Seven leaves out the restroom and walks towards the entrance. He passes the table where he and King sat. He notices that his empty glass of water was now filled. He leans over and takes a couple of sips. While drinking his water, he noticed $50 dollars laying on top of the ticket with writing on it. Seven looks around to see if King could see him. Once he saw no sign of King, he read the words written on the ticket. "Although my brother ate half of his meal without anything to drink, I see something great in you." Seven thought to himself while drinking his water, "she didn't come to check on us one time after we got our food and he still tips her big."

He looks around at the not so busy diner and realizes that he and King were the only two people of color. "Interesting," he thinks to himself while taking his last sip of water. Right before he walks out the diner, he hears a light shout of joy from the waitress who just realized she was tipped big. As Seven walked outside he could see the waitress from the inside pick up the ticket and start reading the message. He then looks ahead and see's the side of King standing at the back of his car smoking a black & mild cigar. Seven silently became a fan of king. He knew he was in the company of a rare individual. You could just feel it the closer he approaches king.

SEVEN: This work vacation. It sounds good, but I can't just drop what I have going here. If I leave now, when I come back I would be evicted from my apartment and fired from my job.

KING: (Takes a drag of his black & mild while thinking before his reacts) You give me the name of your apartments and I'll have Destiny go pay your rent and for next month's rent as well. We still have plenty of time before the office closes. Far as your job, I'll have Destiny call and let them know you have been in an accident and will be in the hospital for some days. You tell me what you make a week and I'll double that for the time you spent away from your job. If they were to fire you, I would make sure all your expenses were paid

• • •

until you found another gig. This will be your time to either relax by doing nothing but ride, or work on your book. But if you don't like living pay check to pay check, you could take your chances and write a story that could change all of that. You never know.

SEVEN: Well how in the world can I turn that down. And you are down to share your story to where I can pick your brain and ask whatever questions I want?

KING: If that's what it will take in order for you to allow me to show my appreciation.

SEVEN: (Feels the wind breeze pick up a little) Okay. I'm in.

KING: (Shakes Sevens hand) Now were talking. You got yourself a deal.

SEVEN: I say we get started right away with the questions.

KING: Of course. First let me get your apartment information so I can send Destiny over to take care of that rent. Let's talk as we move, time is money. Besides, we need to go get you into some clothes, I'm not gonna be riding around with you in this hospital gown all day.

SEVEN: Sounds like a plan. I say we get right to it.

KING: (While both getting into the car) Took you long enough.

SEVEN: What caused you to give that generous tip when knowing the waitress didn't do a very good job?

KING: (Turns on some Bob Dylan on low) In no particular order. Reason number one, without assumption, just as a possibility.. with us being the only people of color, myself having some gold teeth in my mouth and you wearing a hospital gown on, maybe it was her perception that caused her to stay away from us. So fear. Her perception. Two things that can hold us back from getting what is ours. Our missing out on an opportunity. So now, she will always remember this moment. Which will also remind her of the note I wrote. And it will cause her to be better at what she does by reducing her perception of people before knowing them. Possibly eliminating her perception of black people not being good tippers.

The second reason is I know I will be coming back to this place sooner or later. And the next time I come in here, I will be treated better, possibly even have a little power. Word spreads of who the good tippers are. Money talks in this world we live in. Possibly, that same waitress might be working the next time I return. And I would have been on her mind in positive way from the last time we saw each other. I would have become curious to her. And so this time, her guards will have been let down to a certain degree. And that's when I charm her. She wasn't that bad looking and you never know, she could be a little lonely and curious of what it feels like to be a cougar for a night. She might have always wondered what it was like having a little jungle fever. And we just so caught each other while in heat and was in need of a little attention, if you dig what I'm saying. Besides, you never know, people will do something to your food just because of who you are. So if they know I'm okay people, chances are they will leave my food alone. They might it even put a little more love in the food when making it instead. And another thing, it was time for me to sow a seed anyway.

SEVEN: Clever man. Chess, not checkers I see. And that waitress never would have guessed that you would have left such a generous tip.

KING: Let's just say, she did have a little something against black people. After this, it could cause her to have a change of heart. Never know.

SEVEN: And so you have a heart, but can be savage at the same time. And wait a minute here, you listening to Bob Dylan?

KING: What do you know, I changed two perceptions in the last ten minutes. But yes, Bob.

SEVEN: (Laughing in shock) Bob!

KING: Bob was ahead of his time. I like a good deal of his music, but not all. The first rapper in my opinion.

SEVEN: (While looking out the window) That's crazy, I thought I was the only person to think the same thing. That is some cool stuff man. We just pulled up to a red light. If there were to be a million people to pass by and look at you and have to guess what you were listening to, may be one out of that million would have guessed Dylan. That is pretty groovy right there. So who are you man?

• • •

KING: (Looks at Seven while driving) I am King. Don't you need a pen and some pad? Are a recorder or something.

SEVEN: No, it will all be stored in my mind for now. Sometimes I might jot something down, but for the most part I store it all in my mind until I feel it. Then I'll just go in with the writing or typing.

KING: Roger that.

SEVEN: So I see a young black man with a gold grill jamming some Bob Dylan. So how does that come about? Who was responsible?

King then begins to tell Seven the story. The story went something like this: FLASHBACK

The keys of the prison guard jingle while unlocking the cell door. Fire was in his eyes while standing in front of steel bars. He sees the bottom pair of prison slippers crossed on the top bunk. The steal bars run across his eyes from the door opening. He pauses for a moment and slowly looks up at the tall white guard, then back inside of the cell. He takes two steps in before hearing the door slam shut behind him. He turns around and goes through the process of being uncuffed. He rubs his wrist while staring outside the prison bars. The man who lays on the top bunk has his hands together resting on his chest. He then raises up like the undertaker and calmly speaks.

JOE: What made you do it?

KING: (Turns around and faces the cell) Do what?

JOE: What caused you to do it? Dig deep and think, what was at the core of your decision that landed you in here?

KING: (While walking over to the bunk) Yo, I don't know who you are white man?

JOE: (In a calm way, he raises up and swings his legs off the edge of the top bunk and jumps down to the ground. Then makes eye contact) My apologies, my name is Joe. They call me, Info Joe. Now, I would like to know, what caused you to get yourself in here? And you are going to have to look past skin color, because it's bigger than that.

KING: How easy for you to say white boy.

JOE: I told you my name. It's Joe.

KING: (Slowly steps up face to face with anger in his eyes) You want problems old man!

Joe sends a quick punch to the solarplex of King and folds him up gasping for air. In the mist of gasping for air, Joe embraces him and gracefully speaks in his ear, "breath, deep breath young lion." Joe slowly guides the gasping King to sitting on the edge of the bottom bunk. While trying to catch his breath, King gives Joe an evil look as if he was in for it once he catches his wind.

JOE: You are going to have to learn self- control young

● ● ●

man. Now let's talk while I make you hot tea.

KING: (While still catching his breath) You should have killed me.

Joe swiftly moves his whole face 3 inches away from the face of King. His eyes are wide open to its max as if he had just won the lottery. His green eyes are dead locked in with a desperation look before he responds back to King.

JOE: Do it! Pleeease do it! Do it for me, take me out of this misery. Please, I'll give you all my tea's and goodies. Hmm but if you kill me, you may not receive the message. And since they call me Info Joe for a reason, there will be a lot of angry people outside of these bars if you harm me.

While King looks like he had seen a ghost. Joe then cool, calm and collectively eases away from the face of King and climbs to his top bunk. Once in comfort, he didn't move an inch. King looks like he just saw a real live monster when realizing his new roommate was crazy. Joe had touched his soul like no other. With both fear and curiosity, he had never been handled like that before. Revenge was in his eyes. No way was he going to let him get away with it. He moves from the bottom bed and slowly rises up to be eye level with Joe. Soon as he lifts high enough to make eye contact with Joe, he realized that Joe was already prepared for him. Joe was laid stretched out on his side with one hand holding the side of his head up. Joe had a look as if nothing had ever happened.

JOE: Would you like you some tea?

KING: (He then looks helpless like he just gave up. He leans his head up against the top bunk) Maan who are you man?

JOE: It's okay young lion. I'll make us some tea. You sit down and relax and will talk. You probably haven't ate in hours. Do you like honey buns?

KING: (In a look of total confusion and a brief moment of silence) Your serious aren't you? (A brief moment of silence) Yea.. yea man, I like honey buns.

JOE: Great, I love herbal tea with a honey bun. It's a damn good combination.

While Joe prepares the tea, King slowly gains his full wind back while contemplating if he should stomp the old man out or not. He sizes him up. Joe weighed a buck sixty and stood 5 foot 9 inches tall. Small but thorough. He wore a straight face. His eyes gave a feel of wisdom that stemmed from sorrow. He moved without making much noise. Joe slowly turns around towards an angry looking King while handing him a warm cup of tea in one hand and a honey bun in his other hand.

JOE: Ten out of ten times you would whoop my ass in a fight. So understand that in your mind, lose the pride young lion. The question you have to ask yourself is this, "why am I here?" Just maybe you and I are supposed to meet. And me being one who calls a spade a spade, I cut out all beat around the bush talk out and get right to it. So forgive me for being so frank.

KING: Love... Love is why I am here.

JOE: Well I'll be, how interesting is that. And so I tell you, forgive any person who you feel is at fault and forgive yourself and move on from it. Let it go. The question is now, what are you going to do from here on out? And when you get out, what will you become. Will you be a modern day slave? Or will you become the king that you are?

Joe lifts his cup toward King and makes a toast, "to a new beginning." King doesn't respond by lifting his cup, instead he just looks at the older man. Joe acts as if he touched cups with an invisible person and takes a sip of his tea.

JOE: I may move a little fast, but we may not have much time. Perhaps the law of attraction brought you here. I had a feeling someone like your self will be crossing paths with me soon. Without physically seeing you, I felt your energy and presence. I felt your youth, as if you still had a chance. Then once we made eye contact, I saw fire in your eyes. Look son.

KING: I'm not your son, I don't have a dad.

JOE: I understand, I'm sorry it won't happen again. And their lies one of the root problems.

KING: What's that?

JOE: You don't have a dad. The void. The built in anger that will eventually have to be let out at one point or another. The rebellion. The list can go on and on of what a son may lack or what it may cause psychologically. I'm willing to bet more than 75% of men locked inside this cage lacked love from their father at a crucial time of their lives.

KING: How could you have a child and have nothing to do with it. What kind of real man would do that?

Joe: Well, I can answer that because I'm one of those guys. You meet this woman you love, you don't plan it, but she gets pregnant. And before she has the child, you do dumb shit that gets me locked up in here. Things happen. Knowing that I have a son out here in this world and not knowing who he is or what they are about. It's like going through life missing an arm or leg. I can't speak for all, but for me that is what it's like. Picture you being able to cry at any moment of the day from just the thought of it.

KING: Do you know each other?

JOE: No, I never met or saw him. I don't even know what he looks like. His mother and I totally lost contact. I went missing and one day she finds out I was in prison for a long time. She didn't bother keeping in touch. I don't blame her. Well, to be honest, I don't know if that is true. I don't know if something happen to her. Once I get out of here I plan on searching for him.

KING: You tried to keep in contact with him.

JOE: I tried and tried. After so many times I just stop trying. So any time I get locked up with a young man like yourself, I kinda have the tendency to look out for them. As my way of making up for not being in my own son's life. But I have to feel it ya know. I am not just casting my pearls to swine to anybody. And I felt it with you young man. And if you hear me out, I'll show you how to get out of here better than how you came in. I can show you how to make a lot of money once you get out of here. That's if you make it out.

That was first time King has ever felt love from an elder man. Where it felt genuine. He never would have guessed that it came from a white man. King acted like he still had his guard up, but he really took a likening to Joe. The same day King met Joe, there was prison lock down where the inmates had to stay in their cell for two days from a massive prison riot. This is where Joe wasted no time in teaching him the game in prison. How to survive, who to watch out for, who not to deal with. All the in's and out's and how they can be translated in the free world. King ate all the information up. He became the student while allowing Joe to become to teacher.

 Before prison, Joe was a small time musician and part time con artist when his funds got low. He ran away from home at the age of fourteen and bounced around as a drifter. He would play his guitar in the streets for money. So one day an on looker passing by, asked him to play at his hole in the wall joint. The crowd enjoyed Joe to where people started asking when the next time he would be back. So much to where the owner offered him a job playing music there. The pay wasn't much but it paid the bills. The money he earned caused him to live in the lower income parts of town. Joe was the one white guy in the neighborhood. Overtime he became highly respected by the black people in his community. When things got rough financially for Joe is when the con artist in him pulled him in the wrong crowd. Although he was no longer hurting for money, he was taking risk's that would eventually end up right where he was at. Laying on a top bunk in a dark cell. There lied a young King laying in the bottom cell with his arms folded behind his head.

KING: Joe... Joe... (No answer)

JOE: (Removing his headphones from his ears) Did you call me?

KING: Yes. What are you listening to?

JOE: How rude of me. Would you like to hear some music? Little bit a Bob Dylan, Marvin Gaye, Miles Davis and Coltrane.

KING: Yea that's cool.

Joe secretively cherished the moments when he can talk about music. He took the headphones out of the tape player and turned the volume up so it would play out loud. The two would sit up and talk music while it played in their cell. The two built a strong bond in a short amount of time. When the inmates were off lock down, King stayed by Joe's side and became a sponge. They spoke during chow time as King could feel the eyes come his way from being the new kid on the block.

Instead of going on the yard, Joe wanted to speak to King in the library. While walking through the library.

JOE: Look around King, tell me what you see.

KING: People reading and some searching for a book.

JOE: Right. Either searching or reading. Knowledge is power young man. Gain it. Utilize it. What else to do you see in here?

KING: Older folks.

JOE: That's it, the older folks. The ones who has been there and done that. Less drama goes down in here. (Walks over to the window where you could see outside to the prison yard) Look out there King. Now, really look and open your eyes and see. You know what I see when I look out there?

KING: What do you see?

JOE: (Both staring out the window into the prison yard) I see male ego's, pride, fear, testosterone and unhappiness all covered up by masking it through lifting weights and getting bigger. Getting stronger, getting yoked up. Why? Fear of losing. Fear of getting your ass whopped. Who is the biggest, who is the baddest. Who can look the toughest to where they hope nobody will mess with them. Look, what else do you see? Hanging out talking. You want to go hang out and talk?

KING: No, I don't.

JOE: Playing basketball. You trying to go to the NBA?

KING: No

JOE: Alright, is basketball, or handball, or soccer ball going to lead you anywhere once you leave these prison walls? That's not everybody on the yard. Some are working out to stay in shape and burn time. Burning time by working on your body is good, but why not burn that time on your mind. When you are in your cell, work out your body and get it strong. It's what you do when nobody is around to watch. It's when your alone King. There will come a time when you become real alone and therefore you must possess mental strength to overcome. That is what will determine the rest of your life. The fight you have in your mind. So you see this library, this is where you want to spend most of your time while in this prison.

KING: I understand.

JOE: (Looking at King in the eyes) King, I'm giving everything to you straight now. Your new in here. And this place is full of vultures. There are people right now plotting to see how they are going to test you. There is somebody right now pulling up your name on the computer to see what crime you committed to get in here. You can't see it but it's happening. Sooner or later, they are going to come and test you to see where your heart is at. And if you don't show heart, your days in here can be a living hell.

KING: Oh I'll show heart.

JOE: I know you will young lion. Because you have a lot of anger in you. But what I am trying to get you to see is, you can channel that anger into something positive. You must work on mastering yourself. That is by having your pride and ego under control. Discover what you are good at and beat on that craft daily. Everyone in here will eventually be tested, but by using your mind, you can save yourself a lot of trouble.

KING: There is no escaping it, I know it's coming.

Joe: That is so King. Once they see you have heart, you will have way less problems in here. Learn the game of chess, because that will show you how to think. You don't want to be caught off guard by one of these giant bullies with no stamina or strength. So when you are in that cell, get your strength and conditioning in. Run in place, get your core right and get your legs strong. Come here, look outside this window.

KING: What I'm I looking for?

JOE: You see that big cock diesel man standing there by the bench press? The big 6 foot 6 inches 250 pounds of solid muscle.

KING: Yea I see him.

JOE: They call him Rambo. Look how much power he has. Look at all those guys that fear him. You can sense it. That guy is running the yard. And you want to stay clear of him. If he senses fear, he will salivate at the mouth and seek to devour.

KING: What's an example of how you would play chess to get you out of trouble?

JOE: Ok, one example. When I first met you. You wanted to take my head off. So I had to think quickly. You lost your self -control, so I used that against you. As you waited to see if I was going to match your aggression, is when I used that split second to catch you off guard and be first to act. You are bigger and stronger with youth on your side, so I needed to hit you in a spot that would take your strengths away. For all I know, you could be a bully. And if so, I needed to show you that I didn't fear you to psych out your ego. And tell you something that would get you to think in order to calm you down. If I wouldn't have been playing chess, you possibly could have been running our cell by now.

KING: (Smiling) Damn, you sure did old man. Well congratulations, your the first person to ever handle me like that.

JOE: Whoa wait a minute, is that a smile I see?

KING: (Trying to fight his smile and make a straight face) Yea something like that I guess. That was just cold blooded how you did me.

JOE: Aw it's nothing, happens to the best of us. Look King, I see something in you kid. Vision the life you want in your mind and focus on it. Become obsessed with it. And keep your eyes on the prize. I'll see you in a little bit alright.

KING: Alright. I'll be up in a couple hours.

JOE: Alright kid.

King checked out a couple of books and returned to his cell an hour later. He was eager to get back and talk with the Info Joe. Once he made it back to his cell, he witnesses guards cleaning out some of Joe's things. "What's going on, where is Joe?" "Joe has been moved. He will be transferring to another location."

Silent hurt pained the heart of King. He didn't love much, but when he did, he loved hard. The void of never having that older male take him under his wing was finally there for three days, then gone. Back to being alone in familiar territory. King definitely didn't want to be locked up, but it wasn't so bad with Joe around. He knew that he would possibly never see Joe again. King became hopeless, drained and miserable from facing his reality. The guards finished moving out the rest of Joe's belonging's and King enters the cell by himself. He held in his tears of frustration and anger. He didn't want anybody to walk by and see that he was crying. Emptiness was the word that best described King.

The next day King went to the chow hall alone. He sat by himself at the end of a table. He could feel the tension of other inmates smelling fresh blood. His blood pressure raised high. His self- control was out the window. He felt like exploding from not wanting to be around any human beings. He didn't want to see or be around anybody. After eating he made his way up the library where he stood in the same window and watched out into the prison yard. He watches the bully of the yard named Rambo dominate a conversations. Anger filled in the eyes of King before he turns away from the window and leaves the library.

King walks outside on the prison yard cool, calm and collectively. He walked in the middle of the yard where everyone could see him and just stands there. He stood there for about a minute while looking at the ground in front of him. Then looks up to the sky. Inmates started to watch King stand there. He then looks around and spots out the big 6 foot 6 inch giant. Rambo was minding his own business before King walked in front of him. Soon as Rambo noticed King, he gave him a crazy look as if he was lost.

KING: You gotta light?

RAMBO: Do what?

KING: I said do you gotta light?

RAMBO: Do it look like I gotta light bitch.

Soon as Rambo finished his sentence, King cocked back and hit Rambo with a straight right that was packed with all his life's pain in it. Once the right fist connected to the jaw of Rambo, it left him in a daze. King didn't give him time to think, he then hopped right back on Rambo by catching him with two solid body shots to the rib cage that sent Rambo to one knee. He clutches his stomach while looking towards the ground. That's when King finished him off with a vicious upper cut to the face that left the giant flat on his back. King put his foot on the neck of Rambo, "I said do you gotta light....

bitch!" All you could hear is marching boots in a prison yard of silence.

While King stood over Rambo, a gang of prison guards bum rushed and tackled him to ground. They roughed King up before tying him up, "you think you are going to come in here and cause trouble," while hitting him in the side with their batons. Allowing their elbow to slip down to his jaw. A soccer kick to the thigh and chin checked while being dragged off the prison yard. They took King straight to the hole where he would spend the next three months of his life in solitary confinement. A group of guards dragged Seven in the room from not being able to stand on his own to two feet. The last guard to leave out of the room left the beat up King a message, "let's see how tough you are in there kid, your about to look the demon in the face now. And you better hope Rambo gets moved or dies before you get out of here (Small sarcastic laugh). "Damn, it would suck to be you. Good luck kid," and closes the door shut. The turning point of King's life took place while in the dark and cold room. There was only a hard bed, toilet and a sink inside. There was a small opening that allowed a small amount of light inside. The narrow window he would not be able to see out of from it being up toward the ceiling.

King laid on the side of his face with blood from his mouth dripping on the cold concrete floor. The beat up, angry, hurt young man would spend the next twenty - three hours out of the day inside this room with no human contact for the next three months. His mind was tested to the max. He shouted at the guards through the small opening in the door. He would beg and plead with the guard who dropped off his food at the door to open the door so they could fight. The guards would intentionally forget to take King outside for his one hour out of the hole just to show him who was running things. Sometimes his meals would be missing the meat off the plate. Other days the vegetables. Often they wouldn't take him to shower until he began to calm down.

The young lion King became broken down to where he was losing his mind. His energy for life was running low. He became mad at God. For a moment he became a killer in his mind. He felt what it was like to have a demon spirit in him. He began hallucinating while in the dark room. As days passed he began hearing the phone ring from across the room and would race to it, hoping it was Destiny. He thought he saw demons and angels in a war above him as he curled himself in a ball. He closed his eyes when seeing things. His mind played tricks on him as he began think of checking out of life each day that went by. After he became mad with God, his depression slowly moved into insanity. He contemplated how he could find a way to kill himself.

Just when King was at his worst, while on the way to self- destruction, a package was slipped into the open space of the door. King was so out of it, he just stared at the package on the floor for five minutes before walking over to pick it up. He sat on his bed while opening the package. Inside was Joe's tape player, headphones and few tapes. King laid in his bed in the same position as Joe used to do. Inside were a total of four tapes. The tape already inside the tape player was the album, "What's going on," by Marvin Gaye. The second tape was a mix of Bob Dylan songs. The third tape was the album, "Kind of Blue," by Miles Davis. Last but not least, the fourth tape was a voice recording of Joe. As soon as King put the tape in and pressed play he heard Joe's voice, "If you are hearing this, then that means you have received it. All I know in life is pretty much music, money and the field of con artistry which involves knowing a great deal about the human mind. So since that's all I have to offer, this is what I have to give. Hopefully you can leave out whatever info is not for you, and keep what you can benefit from."

King listened to the tape of Joe speak over and over while soaking in all the information. He was learning from a master people reader and wise hustler. Joe spoke on how to increase your awareness and intuition from reading body language. How to spot out the real from the fake. How he will be able to tell if the woman is your life partner or not. He spoke on how to make money and how to manage it. The importance of patience, persistence and self -control. Joe would tell king in the recording to read the books on Malcom X, Dr. Martin Luther King Jr., Bruce Lee, Jesus Christ, Nat Turner, Muhammid Ali and list of book's to read. King listened to this tape so much that he memorized it all in three days.

The package provided strength and hope to King. He

started working out while listening to the music. He ran in place, did push up's, sit up's and squat's. His body began to get more muscular and define. His mind was becoming sharp, aware and still. The music would take his mind off the misery. Slowly but surely, King was finding himself. He searched from within and became stronger by the day. By the time he was let out of consolatory confinement, King was a new man. Still with fire in his eyes, he was more mature and humbled to go along with a kind of body the ladies love. On his way out of the hole, a guard spoke to king, "bitter sweet news. I recken you would want to hear the sweet part first from being locked up in the dark cage all of this time. The sweet part is, lucky for you, big Rambo was transferred just a couple of days ago. But the bitter part, your man Joe was released into the free world." King was at a different place mentally to where neither bit of news bothered him. He became a better man. He also became cold and numb to feelings. He was a man on a mission and you could feel it through his piercing brown eyes.

The first time King walked out on to the prison yard you could feel the respect he now had. The word spread like wildfire after King took out Rambo. The power that Rambo once had, was now shifted to King just like that. The new inmate who played the role of David slaying the Goliath. At the same time, faced being in the hole for three months like a man, he come out the hole mentally and physically stronger. King looked around the yard and could see and feel the respect from the inmates. Although, he was still behind bars, he mentally knew right then and there, that he has arrived. He would due his time by never being tested. He spent most of his time in the library reading books and listening to music. He gained as much knowledge, wisdom, understanding and game while he was in prison. Soon as he got out into the free world, he was prepared to execute immediately.

BACK TO THE PRESENT TIME:

KING: And that's how I end up listening to Bob Dylan.

SEVEN: Yo, that's some deep stuff man.

KING: Oh were just getting started my light skin brother.

SEVEN: It's all starting to make sense.

KING: Let's go pick up the last items you need to pack. Then go meet up with the one and only, Destiny June.

Chapter

5

DESTINY'S WORLD

The gap in between middle class and poor was the type of houses in the neighborhood King rides through. Seven was learning quickly that King went out of his way to receive as little attention as possible.

KING: There are only two people who has ever been to my home. And those are my clients I sell to. You will be the third. I'm sure Destiny will get you all squared away with a pillow and blanket when you decide to get some rest.

SEVEN: Respect. It's all greatly appreciated. So what makes a man who doesn't trust many, allow two drug addicts in his home. I've never heard of that one.

KING: Have you ever been around a functioning addict?

SEVEN: Not until I moved into the apartments I currently live. But no one personally.

KING: It's a small world. The apartments you live in used to be my old stomping ground. But to answer your question, it's a feel. An addict may be the most honest person you come by. Good people who just happened to be on that issue. We need each other. I have the fix they need and they bring me the money.

SEVEN: A win win situation.

KING: I wouldn't say that. I find it hard to win when I'm helping them deteriorate themselves. Seems kind of twisted. Speaking of the devil, there they go, Squint and Turtle HAHA.. These two joker's will have you laughing your ass off. Like two uncles I never had.

SEVEN: Why do they call him Squint and Turtle?

King: Because he always squinting his eyes like something stink. He wears glasses but he can't keep up with them. I stopped buying them after the third pair he lost. So now he just buys the cheapest pair he can see out of from the dollar store. I might see him walking down the street in some glasses with thick purple frames. Or some tiny glasses where the frames are like half an inch. You know the ones they let rest on their nose. Something like Benjamin Franklin would wear while writing a letter. He usually just goes without. And far as Turtle, hell, his name speaks for itself, he slow. Straight auto pilot. He has one speed, cruise control. He talks with a very slow pace although pretty witty.

King turns into the drive way and both Squint and Turtle were standing on the porch watching the car drive in. They get out of the car with bags in their hand and walked towards the front porch.

KING: I just know I'm seeing things. Why am I pulling up and seeing two old ass men standing here, looking like they just came from a Salvation Army swap meet extravaganza.

TURTLE: We knocked on the door but no answer.

SQUINT: Salvation Army got some bad ass shit in there, what you mean?

KING: Yall know the script.

SQUINT: Destiny didn't answer the door, what you want us to do?

KING: Go sit in the car, leave, do something besides sit at my front door.

TURTLE: We just got here, been sitting for about thirty seconds, tops.

SQUINT: Ohhh the feds is watching twenty-four hours a day from a satellite in sky looking ass.

KING: Squint where is your glasses at? What happen this time?

SQUINT: Man look man..

TURTLE: Yep, go on and tell 'em HAHA.

● ● ●

SQUINT: Damn Bill Cartwright, are you going to let me speak?

TURTLE: You sho right.. well the stage is yours, show us what you got.

SQUINT: It was a lil miscommunication with the manager at Boogie's Chicken Shack. When he grabbed ahold of me, my glasses fell off and they broke.

TURTLE: He lying his ass off!

KING: What happen then T? (King would call Turtle T for short)

TURTLE: Pass the mic one time. We placed an order at Boogie's Chicken Shack right, high on that shit. This crusty ass Squint, damn near ordered the whole menu. He ordered a family size box of boogie's chicken, a box of fries, a box of rolls, pecan pie, corn on the cob, fried pickles and ordered two dozen gizzards.

SQUINT: It was one dozen of gizzards!

TURTLE: So he walks up to the counter and the man tells Squint his total. Remind you, I drove up to the chicken shack with this fool. He didn't have a care in the world. He ordered his food with confidence and rode proudly to the shack with a for-certain look on his face. Walked in and waited in line as if everything was going to be fine. So he gets to the counter and tells them his name on the order. So, soon as they come with all the food is when Squint pulls out his bill fold. Tell me why he pulls out four dollars and some lose change that was down in the bottom corners of the bill fold. Then held the money out in his hand. To make a long story short, the man behind the counter stuck his hand out to the east, and swung it to the west, and slapped the dog shit out of Squint. That slap slid him under a table. His glasses flew and all you heard was loose change hitting the ground. From the time he got pimped slapped, until the time he slid under the table. He managed to still be holding those four dollar bills sticking up in the air.

KING: (Laughing) How long was he down for the count T?

TURTLE: Oh he was outta there passed the ten count. Knocked out at the chicken shack for coming in there with that bullshit.

KING: (Laughing) Damn, a slap got you KO'd like that! You didn't eat your wheaties that morning?

SQUINT: Man screw yall, I don't have to take this. (walks off to the car)

KING: O he mad now. (The three watch him walk away) Watch, I bet you he turn around any second.

About five seconds later, Squint turns around and starts walking back towards the porch. One of the laces to his velcro shoes didn't always stay attached, so it would lean over to the ground as he walked.

SQUINT: Look man, let me tell yall something, yall ain't no good.

KING: Yeah, look at him. Forgot what he came over here for in the first place.

SQUINT: Damn right, speaking of that.

KING: Say Turtle, Squint, I want yall to meet Seven.

SEVEN: Hey fellas, nice to meet you guys.

SQUINT: I thought you were an angel when I noticed somebody riding in the passenger seat. Somebody riding with King just don't happen. And I'm just now hearing you speak to, no for real, I thought I was just coming down off a high and was seeing a spirit following King. That's why I didn't speak to you right at first. But pleasure meeting ya.

TURTLE: Just when you think you have heard it all, Bowinkle over here will find some way to surprise ya eveytime. Imma pray for you man. But pleasure to meet you young blood.

SQUINT: Pray for yourself, oh Jimmy the Cricket looking ass.

Seven laughs while King opens the front door. Seven hears the music of Billie Holiday from the back part of the house. Without making it look obvious, Seven was very observant of how King went about his life. King walks through a hanging curtain in front of the hallway entrance to the back part of the house. Turtle was last to walk inside and find him a seat on the couch. Squint looks for the remote and turns on the television. The inside of the home was your typical furniture consisting of your standard things in a living room and kitchen. Nothing out of the ordinary. King returns by walking though the curtain, "Destiny is in the back, she doesn't know we are here, surprise her. Go ahead and go back there."

Seven walks through the curtain and the entire vibe changed. The whole back part of the house was decked out. From typical, to live and vibrant. The ambience, carpet, art work, paintings and the rich taste in the air. A light shined out of the back room. He could smell the scent of a woman as he approached the light. He walks to the door and looks inside. While standing in front of the door, he sees is a silhouette of Destiny high up on a stripper pole. The pole stood from the ground to the ceiling. Her silhouette was spinning gracefully in front of a movie screen that covered the whole wall displaying the movie, Kill Bill on mute. She was unaware that Seven was watching. He felt a slight conviction for standing there while in the moment. The classic sound of Billie Holiday playing while a graceful woman moved with elegance on a pole.

He noticed that Destiny's hair was not long as he remembered. She locked her legs to the highest point of the pole while her shoulders and head leaned away from the pole. She tilted her head back to where she sees the room upside down. She had some small boy shorts on, a cut shirt that leaves her stomach open and a silk robe that dangles from her body. It's like she was on a merry go round in slow motion. Her eyes were closed while spinning. It was like watching a ballerina high up on a pole. Seven didn't want to interrupt her so he stood there and watched her perform. Destiny leaned her back against the pole while upside down. While in motion she opens her eyes and sees Seven. She slowly slides down to the bottom of the pole while still making eye contact. Right before she reaches the bottom, she repositions her body for perfect landing. She stands up and fixes her robe while never taking her eyes off of Seven. The narrow glare coming from the projector to the wall spotlights her face. Her moving in closer felt like a woman goddess was approaching. She walks up to him and places the palms of her hands on both sides of his face.

DESTINY: My angel. I'm so thankful for you.

SEVEN: How are you feeling Destiny?

Destiny: I feel a lot better. It's so good to see you, I didn't know if you were still alive or not. I prayed and prayed that you were okay. How are you doing?

SEVEN: I'm okay. Just a little sore.

Destiny gave Seven a hug and didn't let go until she ready.

DESTINY: Come in, welcome to my world. You caught me in the middle of a work out.

SEVEN: That was wonderful. I have a new appreciation for pole dancers. The music selection made it even more cool.

DESTINY: Well, I'm not a pole dancer, but thanks love. It's great for working out. Strengthens the core. And far as Billie Holiday, I love her.

SEVEN: (While turning his head and looking at the room) This world of yours, I've never seen nothing like it. I wouldn't want to leave this room. It's like a home movie theater room, slash lounge, slash get away spot.

DESTINY: You like it?

SEVEN: Yea it's pretty live in here.

DESTINY: And so I hear your going on a trip with us?

SEVEN: Yea I'll be tagging along.

DESTINY: Yayyy it's going to be so much fun.

SEVEN: Your hair is different.

DESTINY: That was a wig I was wearing last night.

Seven: I love it. It's so different.

DESTINY: Aww, well your just making my night complete. Yea, ya girl be switching it up on them. (patting her hair in a sassy way)

SEVEN: So was that a disguise last night?

DESTINY: Was what a disguise?

SEVEN: That look in your eyes before you ran your finger though my piece of cake without asking, or washing your hands?

DESTINY: You didn't mind. You probably ate that part of cake first.

SEVEN: (Smiles) You think so?

Destiny: (Long pause) Yes it was a disguise. (Before Destiny could finish her sentence King walks in the room)

KING: What's on the menu Destiny. You want me to order something?

DESTINY: Hold what you got. You boys are in for a treat tonight.

KING: Whaaaaat, what you got on your mind.

DESTINY: Seven do you eat meat?

KING: In moderation I do. I keep a balance. A vacation is a good time to enjoy it all.

DESTINY: Ok good, cause I'm thinking fish, chicken alfredo, broccoli and bread sticks. Water with lemon and wine for the drink. How does that sound?

SEVEN: That sounds amazing. I don't know when the last time I ate like that.

KING: Already, that's what I'm talking about, let's eat!

DESTINY: Well I'm about to take a bath, and when I get out, I'll whip that right on up.

(King and Seven leave out from the back room and rejoin Turtle and Squint)

KING: So are yall getting ready to leave, or trying to stay and get beat on them dominoes.

TURTLE: Aw here we go again. You see Seven, I can't fool with them no more, they both been lying their ass off all day.

SQUINT: I hear you talking youngster, but I don't hear no dominoes being washed.

KING: Yall turn the game on mute and come on over here. Seven, I put a towel, wash cloth, soap, and all that good stuff in the bathroom back there. Or if you want to get in the mix, hey, it's your world.

SEVEN: Cool, I'll go shower up, then come back and get in the mix.

KING: Already then author, sound like a plan. Besides, you been asking all the questions. Now it's time for me to get to know who you are.

SQUINT: King you wouldn't happen to have any cold brew's sitting up in that ice box would ya?

TURTLE: Hello, that's what I'm talking about. Squint, I don't know why King acting all brand new.

KING: HaHa, yea I have some beer in there. But I'm charging.

SQUINT: Aw hell naw!

KING: I'm a business man, what do you mean.

TURTLE: I'm out then man. I just got a little tired all the sudden.

SQUINT: Yea me to, maybe some other time.

KING: (Laughing) Oh it's like that huh, alright. (Looks at Seven while smiling as his gold teeth were shinning) You see how they do me? Yea I got some beer in the refrigerator for yall, free of charge.

Seven leaves for the back while Squint and Turtle helped themselves to some beer. King turns on some music and breaks out the dominoes. The sound of pots and pans clinging together in the kitchen was Destiny preparing to throw down. When Seven returned back, he felt like he was entering a room of a close nit family. Destiny looked stunning in the most simple way. It was the third time Seven was in her presence and there was three different versions of her almost. This time she looked like your everyday girl in her jeans and t shirt. The cool pretty woman at your job who everybody liked for not letting her beauty go to her head.

When she walked over and placed a glass of wine next to Seven. He gravitated to her scent without making it look obvious. She washed her hair so it was still a little damp and smelling good. Her nails were done, her skin was glowing, while wearing no makeup. She was hard not to like. Despite Sevens understanding of how dynamite she was, he had no plan of doing anything he wouldn't want his girlfriend to do. Not to mention her big brother being King.

Seven took score of the domino game, while he sat back taking in the new experience. He would never have guessed that he would be sitting at a table with a hustler, two functioning drug addicts and an intriguing woman who happens to be a virgin in the kitchen cooking a home cooked meal. Seven learned more about King from all the music being played from his phone. The more Turtle and Squint spoke, the more it was understood that you can never judge a book by its cover. Despite their flaws, they were both OG's in the game who has been there and done that.

Destiny didn't say much. She would chime in here and there. Sometimes use the spatula as a microphone and sing to different parts of songs. Once the food was ready, she made the men their plates and served them at the table. It was new for Seven to be around a woman of such beauty and grace be that down to earth. The pen was working in his mind. His heart was warming up. He began to feel even more alive, while eating the good food Destiny prepared. His appreciation for the smallest of things were noticed by King. The more King scoped Seven out, the more he believed that Seven was as advertised. His writings matched his character.

Once they finished eating, both Squint and Turtle left for the night. King, Destiny, and Seven went to the back room in Destiny's world. There was an area of comfortable seating by the projector screen. The only light in the room was coming from her fish tank and the old school Pam Greer movie the plays from the projector.

KING: How you feeling Seven?

SEVEN: I feel good. I'm truly appreciative of all the love and hospitality. I haven't ate like that in a long time. Or have I laughed like that in a while. Besides my body being soar, I feel good.

KING: It's all our pleasure my brother.

Destiny tells Seven to come sit on the floor in front of her and lean his back against the couch. The feel wasn't in a flirtatious way. It was more of a reaction when someone you care for is in need. Seven was a bit hesitant until looking at King who didn't look as if he was against it. He followed her wishes and sat were she asked him to. Both Destiny and Seven now sat across from the man thinking of a master plan. King didn't change his expression at all from fully trusting his sister's ability to know what she was doing. Destiny massaged the shoulders, neck, and a part of the upper back of Seven while they listened to King speak.

KING: Flying is too risky. I'm thinking road trip. There is a big Mayweather fight in Las Vegas this weekend so the traffic will be crazy. Little bit of gambling, little bit of shopping, and eat good. We could hit the Cali coast, put our feet in the sand and just live it up.

DESTINY: Do slipper's count on this vacation?

KING: The karmetic train is coming indeed. You know the drill.

DESTINY: And you know I stay ready to be a blessing.

SEVEN: Sounds like one great experience awaiting to happen. I'm here for the ride.

KING: It's a done deal then. We can leave in the afternoon to give us a few extra hours of rest. I would advise you my wise man, just go for the ride. The time is now.

SEVEN: I'm with it.

The trio sat around and talked a little more before King shakes Seven's hand and leaves the room. Destiny finishes up her massage and sits down on the floor next to Seven. The two look forward at the 70's movie playing on the projector screen.

SEVEN: Thank you. I already feel the difference.

DESTINY: Your welcome.

SEVEN: For the first time in years I felt like I was at a family get together. This is all new to me.

DESTINY: Yea it's our little circle. Turtle and Squint come over and hang out sometimes but that is it. You must have really took an effect on him because he doesn't call anybody his brother. You know what that means right?

SEVEN: No, what does that mean?

DESTINY: Once he calls you his brother, you are in. You have someone who will really ride for you.

SEVEN: Under the outer layer, I sense a lot of good in that heart of his.

DESTINY: There is. Not too many have experienced that side. I remember when we were kids, he was just different. Off in his own world. We would walk home from school with all the kids who lived in the same apartment. He would walk off from the pack, although he was with us. There was this back alley that we would have to pass in order to make it home. And one of the houses we passed had a fence with this huge dog. That ugly dog would jump on the top of the fence and just bark at us like crazy, like it wanted to get over that fence and tear us into pieces. The dog's neck and face would be sticking out from the top of the fence. Our little gang of kids would run passed the dog fast as we could. One kid would cry, while some would act like they were getting ready to have an anxiety attack before we passed Cujo. So one day we were running past the dog and I fell to the ground. King and some of the other kids picked me and carried me a little further from the barking dog. Once King saw that I scraped my elbow and it was bleeding, I saw that look in his eyes. That look will clear a room out if they knew what was good for them. As I was sitting down and looking up towards the sky, the whole group of kids were huddled over me to see if I was okay. I could see King standing there looking down at me with revenge in his eyes. You could hear the dog barking like it was possessed by the devil. King then turned around and stared at the barking dog from a distance.

SEVEN: The plot thickens.

DESTINY: So King stands there with his fist balled up, while the other kids are helping me up to my feet. King started walking towards the dog. We were yelling at him to come back. But he just kept walking towards that beast. I was scared out of my mind, I thought Cujo was going to eat my brother. Once King got close to the dog, he turned and looked the dog face to face. That vicious dog was barking like crazy to where spit was flying out its mouth but King didn't show any signs of fear. The dogs head looked twice the size of Kings. There they stood looking each other in the eyes. This is when I feel like everything changed. King took a step forward at the dogs face that was leaning over the fence, and cocked his fist back and punched the dog right in his it's nose.

Seven: Whaaat!

DESTINY: Yes! The dog squealed and backed off of the fence. The dog became scared of King. And we didn't hear another sound from the dog. All of the kids started cheering like we just won a championship game as King walked back towards us. The kids lifted King up on their shoulders and they carried him off to our apartments. You should have seen the look on his face, it's the happiest I've ever seen him.

SEVEN: Hey that's cool right there. Straight out of a movie scene.

DESTINY: But check this out, the next day at school on our way home, the dog just watched us, never heard another bark from that dog again. That's when King gained so much respect. He had a reputation as a child.

SEVEN: He has a dominating presence to him.

DESTINY: Ever since that day, I just totally trusted my brother. And since we didn't know our bi- logical parents, he became like my father.

SEVEN: You and King were adopted too? I mean I knew my mother, but I was eventually adopted.

DESTINY: We didn't have the same father but we were always in each others lives. They say King's father died of a drug over dose. My father just left and nobody ever heard from him again. Our mother passed away when we were babies so we never really knew who she was.

SEVEN: (Shaking his head) My goodness. I can't even imagine that. My mom passed away from cancer when I was eleven. But to have lost both parents had to been tough.

DESTINY: It definitely took its toll.

SEVEN: So, who is Destiny June? So far from what I've seen, I mean, what can't you do? We entered each other's lives less than a day ago and I've witnessed you cook, thrill me with your pole dancing, massaged pain out of my body, do poetry on the fly, serve plates of food, listen to Billie Holiday and have three different looks. And not to mention, read parts of my mind. And I'm sure there is a lot more to add. Who on God's green earth are you?

She turns from watching the Pam Greer fighting scene and looks at Seven. She gently rubs the outside of her hand against Seven's wound above his eye brow.

DESTINY: Who am I? I'm still trying to figure that out. I can be that girl from the hood. I can be that sweet southern bell. I can be that educated and independent woman. I can be your everyday girl. I can be a bad bitch with money. I can have a man's soul at my mercy. I can do all these things but I'm not complete. Nor have I been in true love. Or have I made love. And last night was a wake up call.

SEVEN: A one of a kind you are. Being a virgin in today's world has become extinct. How have you managed to do so?

DESTINY: I have to give my brother King a great deal of credit for that. His communication with me was like a big brother, father, teacher, and friend. One day he asked me what I wanted to be in life. What was my dream? After I told him, he dedicated a part of his life to help me reach that dream. Using my body as a temple being one of them. He taught me the game. He brought me inside the mind of your average man. He believes that the power of sex is one of the main reasons to cause distractions. That sex was one of many big reasons people do not achieve their dreams.

SEVEN: How so?

DESTINY: One day you are free and ambitious. Then you fall in lust, or maybe seasonal love and become sexually active. Then you slip up and have kids. Which is a 24 job. So how many are going to have the same drive or energy to put towards their dream after having kids? The dream seems to fade away, and we end up settling. Or going with the best paying option. So King was like, why not take care of my business first, have my life in order, then start thinking about a relationship. He tells me that sex is like a powerful drug that can be addictive. And once you become a part of it, it can change the dynamics of our thinking and effect our decision making. So when it comes to a partner, until we get that feeling inside that we can't describe, it's not the time to entertain it.

SEVEN: Big bro taught you well. Have you had any boyfriends?

DESTINY: Yea I had a couple. Mostly just going on a date here and there. Once I let them know I'm not having sex, they eventually fade off over time. Some think they can change your mind, or some try to hang in there long as possible, but not long enough. The one who is willing to wait for me is the one who really loves me for me. Strange how a man like my brother can plant the right seeds to somehow get me to save myself for the one I wouldn't mind being with forever.

SEVEN: Righteous. I'm impressed. What does King teach or instil that most parents may fail to do, or to realize? Because a parent can only do so much.

DESTINY: Time. He realized at an early age, there was no way he could properly raise me the way he wanted to by working most of day. The minimum wage he was making wasn't enough. That's when he started looking towards the streets to make fast money. It didn't take him long to start making money because he already had a reputation. Not only from having respect in the streets, but from playing ball. He was an awesome basketball player, easily could have went D1 but he chose the streets. Going to college wasn't going to make him money to help support us. Eventually the life style took its toll on him. He got tired of being on call 24/7 and taking having to take cat naps. He still had to get me to school and everywhere else. He was spending more time making money to provide, then actually being with me. That is when he started to find ways to get money without having to spend so much time to make it.

SEVEN: The beginning stages of becoming a mastermind to create that time.

DESTINY: That's right. That is when he activated the power of his name, King. He devoted his time into me. He helped me with my homework. If he didn't know how to do it, he would find someone who did. He would drive out to the rich neighborhoods and ride pass the big houses. He wanted to show me something different than what I was accustomed to seeing. He told me that I can have one of these houses one day if I was willing to work hard and stay focused.

SEVEN: Planting those seeds.

DESTINY: That's what he did with a lot of his time. He poured those essential seeds of growth into me. I was the only thing he had in this world. The more he learned, the more he would feed me the knowledge.

SEVEN: How awesome was that, being schooled by your older brother.

DESTINY: Oh but don't get it twisted, it definitely was a challenge. When he went to prison is when he stepped it up even more. After he came out of that hole for 3 months is when everything changed. He would say over and over in his letter's to just trust him. Each letter he sent me, I could feel the growth. I could feel his desire to get out and execute this plan of his. He knew the right buttons to press and get me to dig deep. He gave me a workout regiment, homework assignments and small mission's to complete.

SEVEN: If you don't mind me asking, what kind of homework and missions?

DESTINY: Far as homework, I would have to read certain books and watch certain documentaries. Past greats like Madam C. J. Walker, Nat Turner, Malcolm X, Huey Newton, Harriet Tubman, Angela Davis, Bruce Lee, Nikala Telsa, Maya Angelo and Ali to name of few.

SEVEN: That is a powerful bunch, sounds like he was mentally preparing you.

DESTINY: Yep, the homework was for the mental and the missions were for the physical. The missions consisted of running a certain amount miles per week, exercising and staying on a healthy diet. He knew I was in college so he didn't overdo it. I was just so amazed by his growth, it caused me to believe in my big brother even more. Before I knew it, I was starting to see a change in my body. The working out and eating a proper diet started getting ya girl body right. Had me feeling like a superstar out here. At the same time, all the knowledge and wisdom I was consuming was causing me to grow and mature. It's like my eyes opened, while being totally awoke.

SEVEN: I love it. How lucky am I to be around such one of kind human beings. This is like, the coolest story I've ever heard when combining what I know about you and your brother so far. And I ask myself the question, what landed me here.

DESTINY: Maybe because you are the one.

SEVEN: And what makes you believe your discernment is an accurate judgement. Especially when you or your brother don't know much about me.

DESTINY: It's amazing how our upbringing can mold us to be so humble, to where we are not fully aware of our own self-worth. Which may cause one to not see what others around them can see.

SEVEN: (Turns and looks at Destiny from her words hitting his soul)

DESTINY: Consider yourself blessed. I know the men very well, and it's discouraging to a young virgin woman who awaits true love. And when I am around a man of purity, it's like a breath of fresh air. I believe it is in the book of Matthew 6: 22, "the eyes are the lamp

● ● ●

of the body, if your eyes are healthy, your whole body will be full of light."

SEVEN: I see.. Matthew, the tax collector who left everything to follow Jesus. I guess I never saw what other's saw in me.

DESTINY: A handsome man can take advantage of his looks just as a woman can. When you see one alone on his birthday, at a conscious spot like The Melting Pot, who happens to be courteous and humble, that is rare. If you were to google the word, humble, it would read, "having or showing a modest or low estimate of one's own importance." Synonyms for the word humble are meek, deferential, respectful, submissive, diffident, underprivileged, self- effacing to name a few. And with that being said, my world flashed in front of me. I thought I was going to die, get raped or get me and my brother caught up. I know my relationship with God hasn't been like it should, but I prayed as I lost strength. That man was too strong for me to fight off. And just as I couldn't fight anymore, out of nowhere this man comes and saves me. And for doing so, he was sacrificed and beat, just so I can live and be free. I thought you might have died that night. And less than twenty-four hours later, this very savior stood at my door way. Like he came back alive like Jesus.

SEVEN: (Chills ran through his body as he gives her a priceless look of appreciation. He politely shakes her hand) You saved me, just as much as I saved you.

They both sat on the floor with their back leaned against the couch. He could feel her energy become receptive of the real touch of a man. Destiny took her right pointer finger and traced the veins in his hand. No more words were spoken as the two experienced the moment. Destiny would fall asleep as Seven mentally wrote in his mind. When the time felt right, he awakes her by asking if she wanted to lay on the couch or go to her bed. She climbs onto the couch and positioned herself to her liking. Before leaving the room, he stops and looks back at her. He thought to himself, before knowing who she was, who would have guessed that a woman so fine, gifted, and smart could be so lonely. Lonely for all the right reasons. He thought of how the world always seems to find a way to balance us out.

He leaves Destiny's world and enters the guest room. He lays on the bed while looking up at the ceiling. He puts the hand he shook Destiny's hand with over his face. Her scent was like no other. It had a sweet, fresh and natural smell of a woman's flesh. He wonders to himself, while lying in the grace of her scent, "what was going to happen next?"

Chapter **6**

WHO IS SEVEN?

The smell of breakfast awakes Seven out of his sleep. It took him back to when his mother would have the whole house smelling every Saturday morning. He rolls out of bed and gets on his hands and knees. After connecting to the source, he makes his way to where the smell was coming from. He passes through the curtain and sees King in the kitchen putting the finishing touches on breakfast.

KING: Good morning Mr. Author.

SEVEN: Good morning. It sure is smelling good in here. I wasn't expecting to see you in here cooking it up.

KING: Yea, I can show you better than I can tell you.

SEVEN: Right on.

• • •

KING: You sleep good family?

SEVEN: I slept great. Yo, what kind of bed is that?

KING: It's a therapeutic mattress. If anybody has a problem sleeping on that mattress, then I don't know what to tell them.

SEVEN: That's the most comfortable bed that I ever slept on in my life.

In comes Destiny looking fly, but yet comfortable as she wants to be. She makes the simple things look good. She wore a native Indian head band with her hair in two pig tails coming down each side, a kid Cudi t-shirt and some leggings that brought out the fabulous shape of Miss June. Seven placed his bags by the garage door alongside the other luggage. The trio ate breakfast and began to prepare for take off. King checks to make sure all the windows were locked in the house. Once all the perimeters were secured to his satisfaction he sets the alarm. The alarm system was top of the line, consisting of a burglar blaster. The blaster dispensed pepper spray from triggered movements in certain locations in the home. The whole back yard was set up with movement sensors. A high tech video recording system set up on all four sides of the home. He could watch the outside of his home from on his cell phone. The area he wanted secured most was his small homemade built in closet where he kept his safe.

Both Destiny and Seven walk out into the garage and begin loading their bags in the trunk of King's shiny black Cadillac. Seven always wanted to ride in the back seat of a Cadillac so he left the modesty behind for once and made the move without seeing about the seating arrangements. Destiny got in the front seat and looked at herself in the mirror. King was last to enter the car. Seven admired King's choice of attire. People around his neighborhood would think he was just a quiet guy who might wear a white T-shirt, jeans, Jordan's and driving a everyday car. And that was just how he wanted it to be. But outside of that, King was that fly guy who appreciated looking sharp, well dressed and smelling good.

KING: Alright we know the drill. It doesn't hurt to double check.

DESTINY: Registration, inspection, valid driver's license, insurance are good?

KING: Roger that.

DESTINY: All fluids are topped off, tire pressure and the house alarm is good?

KING: Roger that.

DESTINY: Watchu got for me?

KING: You got the reservations for hotel situated and the ticket confirmations for the Floyd Mayweather fight?

DESTINY: Roger me up big bro. I had to buy the tickets from someone who was selling them online. You know the Mayweather fight tickets been sold out for a while now. But your girl worked her jelly for us.

KING: Where are the seat's located. I need them where all the money is at.

DESTINY: (Looks at King and speaks in a British accent) Are you trying to make a mockery of me. Of course they are. I even managed to get them eleven rows from the ring.

KING: Look at her go! (Shaking his head in disbelief while looking at Seven in the rear view mirror) Seven, this sister of mine never ceases to amaze me.

DESTINY: (Switches her voice to a Puerto Rican girl from the Bronx accent) Thank you Pappi, you know I'm all about the team work to make the dream work.

KING: So we're good to go.

Both King and Destiny turned to the back seat and looked at Seven at the same time.

KING: You ready to rock and roll author.

DESTINY: (Speaks in a seductive school girl tone as if she was in an acting audition) Yea Mr. handsome Author, are you ready to escape with us.

SEVEN: (All smiles) I really don't know what I'm getting myself into, but I'm ready.

KING: That's what I'm talking about. Let's ride! And you are the man with the pen and pad, write away compadre.

SEVEN: Roger that.

DESTINY: Okay okayyy. I don't know big bro, he might be the shitz.

KING: You might be on the same something. We might have a killer back there.

DESTINY: He just don't know it yet.

KING: Or maybe he does know.

DESTINY: In order to push that pen you have to be able to think. And that's what they don't want us to be able to do. I don't know King, could we be dealing with a mastermind back there?

SEVEN: (Placing his pen on the top of his ear and chewing on a piece of gum) Only time will tell.

King signals for the garage door to open and the three amigos take off for Las Vegas.

The pen in Seven's mind is puzzling all the pieces together. The more time Seven spent around King and Destiny is the more he realized how he was witnessing something you only see in movies. Despite how they lived their lives, he felt honored to be around the brother and sister. The were ghost like a CIA agent, mentally sharp as the bank robbers on the movie Oceans Eleven, and just cool as the wind. They genuinely made Seven feel more confident about himself. The young writer stares out the window and views God's creation of earth. The fact of both King and Destiny being music lovers makes the road trip even more satisfying. Only the music played when leaving out of the Dallas/Ft. Worth metroplex. It wasn't until they began to see green pastures and open land before they started conversing. Destiny turns sideways so she could see both King and Seven.

DESTINY: So I hear you are an author.

SEVEN: Well, I'm technically not an author yet. I have some material I'm working on.

KING: Do you write often or ever find yourself writing a little bit every day?

SEVEN: That's an everyday thing. Even if it's just a sentence or two.

KING: Well then, you are a writer despite not having a book published yet. Or if anybody has yet to read your work. That is what you do, that is a part of who you are. So you can claim it as if you are already an author. Own it my brother.

SEVEN: Right on. I feel you on that note.

DESTINY: Read something for us Seven.

SEVEN: I don't have anything on me right now.

DESTINY: What about what you wrote right there on the pad?

SEVEN: Oh this is just some doodling around.

DESTINY: I'm all ears (While seating there staring at Seven in the spacious Cadillac)

KING: He'll eventually come out that shell messing around with Destiny June.

SEVEN: Ok I'll read it. But first do you mind if we play something with a mellow beat.

DESTINY: (While putting the AUX cord in her phone to play an instrumental) How does a Jay Dilla instrumental sound?

SEVEN: That's right down my alley (Seven lifts his pad closer to where he could read better)

"Ever so moments of a bit worried from visions that arrive, possibilities of movies of our lives shaped right in front of my eyes. Listen close to the words on the carved wall of the strangers cell who opens up to tell what is seldomly unveiled. Knowing to go unjudged when it's just us, so out of their shell to peep over their well, for a mental show and tell from the ones who feels of fails and the ones who breaks spells," .. And that's all I have so far on this piece of paper.

Seven and King make eye contact in the rear view mirror for a brief moment while Destiny smiles while nodding her head up and down.

DESTINY: Did you to start writing that since we got into the car?

SEVEN: Yes.

DESTINY: We haven't been driving for long at all. Looks like we have a natural on our hands.

KING: A wordsmith.

DESTINY: Yo! I'm feeling it. The word play is sick, and plus it's pretty deep. If you wrote that in this short amount of time, I just wonder what all you have stored up.

SEVEN: I appreciate the love.

KING: I see you listen well. You took a little bit of information I gave you and turned it an art form of words with your own twist to it. Just as we spoke yesterday, do what you have to do in order to create the books you want to write. With your mind and that pen combined, you got something.

SEVEN: I thank you, means a lot to me coming from you two.

DESTINY: What inspired you to write?

SEVEN: Before my mother passed, I asked her how my father was when he was around. I wanted to know what he on. She said he would sit by the window and write music most of the time.

DESTINY: I love how he gives us little tid bits and leaves the rest for our imagination to run wild. Relax and stay awhile, we have hours until we arrive to our destination.

KING: Told ya man, she'll bring it out of you. Besides, "listen close to the words on the carved wall of the strangers cell who opens up to tell what is seldemly

unveiled, knowing to go unjudged when it's just us." I
believe those are the words of Seven.

SEVEN: Man, yall are good. And correct. So here we go.
That thought of my dad writing, that always stayed in
my mind growing up. It wasn't until I graduated high
school, graduated college, and worked for a company
making what most people consider good money. But I
wasn't happy. I had accomplished everything that was
taught or instilled in me. The American dream you
could say. But something didn't feel right. Something
was missing. One day I woke up, and I'm in the world
of money, business, status, ranks, corporate greed, and
fake love. I'm seeing it all right in front of my eyes and
can't stand it. The pride, the selfishness, the lack of
respect. At the core of intentions was greed, power,
riches and control. I found myself not wanting to sit in
hours upon hours of traffic to go work for these kind of
people. I mean, what was I doing it all for?

I got the car I wanted, or thought I wanted. I had a nice
bachelor pad. Had a fine girl. But I didn't love any of
those things. And I began to see the numbers 11:11 all
the time. To where it just wasn't a coincidence. It's like
it was telling me something. I'm getting more
emotionally detached. I'm starting to really understand
what God meant by, not conforming to the ways of the
world. It's like I woke up out of my sleep. And it hit me
when I realized that I have been conditioned. I had
accomplished these worldly things, but was it apart of
my purpose? I didn't know. So I started to seek and
search to find out who I am, and why I was put here on

earth. And I'm seeing the numbers 11, 111 and 1111 more and more.

The more knowledge and wisdom I gained, the more I realized how programmed we are as a whole. It made me mad when learning about all the lies we have been taught. Which didn't do anything but make it worse. That is when I channeled that frustration into something positive. I just didn't know what. I was slowly becoming a loner and off to myself. I was just in a different space. I didn't trust anybody to talk to. Or when I did, I went over their heads. I just wanted to go and be somewhere else. Everything just seemed so fake to me. Or maybe it was me, maybe I was just lost trying to find myself. And that is when I quit my job. I didn't resign my lease. I didn't try and fancy up my resume and send it everywhere on line, hoping another shady company called.

I began to seek who I am and why I was here. In order to do so, I needed to discover my roots and know my genetic makeup. What all is in my blood. The only thing I knew was that my mother was black and my father was a white. I was adopted by a white family who were good people. They brought me in and gave me the best life possible. I never needed for anything. I had routine dental and doctor checkups. I always had lunch money. I went to summer camps. They had money set aside for my college tuition. Everything was cool, but in doing so, I only saw sprinkles of people who looked like me. When I was a child, I was around black people, once I was adopted, I lived in a white community. There were a few blacks at the school. There were a hand full who lived in the neighborhood. After while I just learned to adjust.

The husband and wife were not able to have children of their own so they adopted me. I was the only child. They treated me as if I was their real child. Bless their hearts, I could tell they received a lot of slack for doing so. They didn't care, they loved me. They put me in a good schooling system. Their thing was education. Education, education, and some more education. Pride yourself in doing great in school so I can get into a good college. As long as I was on that track, I had their support. Once I began to be in search of myself and ask questions is when the disconnection started to take place. I know I disappointed them both. They worked so hard in trying to mold me into who they thought I should be. They didn't understand why I would be tired of living in the rat race. They didn't understand me saying that I wanted to find my true purpose in life. They thought I was on drugs once they found out I quit my job and moved out of my bachelor pad. They didn't understand that none of the material things mattered to me. They believed I just threw everything away that I worked for. And I can't blame them. But it was my life, and was ready to seek beyond the physical.

Once I knocked on the door of my black side. Learned more about my African roots and the history of black Americans is when my eyes began to open. Everything started to make more sense of why the world is the way that it is. This is when I start to understand the power melanin. The power of the seeds planted in the Willie Lynch letter. How generational curses of our ancestors of slaves are still in effect today. It led me to the hidden agenda's in the criminal justice system, the educational system and the work force. Why Malcolm X and Dr. Martin Luther King Jr. wasn't assassinated until after they planned to team up. It began to make sense of why leaders were either murdered or black balled. I learned about all the great inventions of blacks that were stolen and claimed by the oppressor. All these thoughts, questions, and ideas ran heavily on my mind once discovering truth.

The more I discovered, the more I was proud of the fact that I was half black. I wanted to do more to help. I wanted to be apart. I just had this feeling of passion come over me. I was treated fairly when growing up in these white communities, but it always felt like I was missing something. Maybe if it were to be more diverse, but it wasn't. When I would run across a black man at the black hair products section in the store, some would call me their brother when they never met me before. Like I was one of them. That hit me, especially already feeling like an outcast. I knew there was more to it than the way black people were portrayed on television, history books, music, and the news. And I wanted to find out for myself. With that in mind, this is right around the time I started from scratch and moved away. I didn't care what part of town it was in. I didn't care how much money I would make at my next job, just as long it could keep me afloat. I didn't care about status. The only thing I cared about was being consistently happy.

I just wondered off and did what I wanted to do. I had a good size saving so I scratched off a few things on the bucket list. I did nothing for a little bit. I traveled a couple times and cleared my mind. I took naps in the middle of the day. I watched movies in the middle of the day. I went out in remote locations and just chilled there for most of the day. Anything that would take me away from the world. Most of the time I stayed at cheap hotels and motels. It's crazy how fast money can go when you're not having a source of income coming in. Although my peace and freedom were increasing, I was running out of money. I had to find the cheapest apartment and in a location of somewhere I wouldn't mind working. A job that could benefit my new walk in life.

While going on my hunt, I learned that there is the rich, your middle class, and the lower class blacks and I ended up moving to the lower class due to the drastic change in the money I was going to be making. Plus, having no plans of working anywhere that wasn't beneficial to my quest. Where my mind was at, I could care less of where I was living. With that being said, I was denied twice of getting hired at the library near my apartments. The manager told me that I was over qualified, even after I told them I would work for the minimum amount. I went up to the library numerous of times and expressed my desire to have the job and still couldn't get hired. I really didn't want to work anywhere else but there. The library was walking distance from my apartment.

I found myself comfortably alone with no where I really wanted to go. What I was in search for was nowhere in the physical. Music became my best friend. I watched my people outside this project window. My whole view on life changed. I don't know what it is about this window, but I was supposed to see through this apartment window of mine. Although I don't know exactly why I am there in the first place. I just checked out of the world and created my own little one. I started thinking thoughts like, how all the work of artists I like would have to write. The author's I read were called, writers. All the music artists I listen to were writers. My dad would write. What I was seeing out this window of mine, caused me to pick up a pen and start writing. And I couldn't stop because I had so much to get out.

I wanted that library job so bad, I began writing notes on a piece of paper and stuck it on the windshield wiper of the managers car. I would write poetry as if I where Edgar Allan Poe on one note, and in parables on the next. The manager called me one night to my surprise. He asks if I could write him some poetry for this woman he's been trying to get a date with. I asked him a few questions about the woman, filtered it all in and wrote a poetry piece for him. He called me back in a few days and said he has been communicating with her ever since. He tells that he has read many books over the years, and knew I was pretty good. He asked me how long I have been writing and once I told him a month, he finally hired me. Not only did he hire me, but once he found out that I was a good worker, he would eventually give me a key to building.

He said he believed in me the more I left writing's on his windshield. He mentioned how my words connects with the reader's heart. He gave me the keys, and said to learn as much as I want, just as long as I didn't do anything stupid. He believed that I could be a number one best seller one day, so he gave me one golden key to elevate my craft. If the building was closed and I wanted a new book, or needed to do some research is when I took full advantage. As long as I kept writing him poetry for his lady, he was fine with me having a key to the small library building.

My life has changed dramatically from quitting my job. I know what it feels like to barely get by. It does something to you. Having to substitute dishwashing soap for laundry detergent. Hand washing your clothes at times. Having to budget 15 dollars at the grocery store. Having to ride the bus when you are used to driving a highly praised car. Adding water to the soap bottles to make it stretch. Buying the cheapest foods. Not having enough money to go see that movie at the theater. Not being able to get that combo meal at your favorite fast food spot when you want it. Not being able to do anything on holidays and birthdays. It causes you to dig deep. It humbles your pride and ego. It caused me to improvise. It did something to my inner warrior. Then I look out my window and know that many are in the same boat that I am in. And I began to feel the people I'm watching outside this window. I began to understand more. It was all making more sense now. I'm learning more about myself than ever.

DESTINY: That is beautiful Seven. You are on the right path.

KING: The chosen one.

DESTINY: If you don't mind me asking, how did your mother pass away?

SEVEN: The same way your mother passed, cancer.

KING: And the plot thickens.

All three become quiet from doing the math in their minds. Their mothers passed from cancer and all three were adopted. You could feel the energy of the heavy thoughts of all the possibilities of how they came together.

SEVEN: I believe I have obtained enough information that can get rid of cancer, and many other illnesses. Over the years I've done a lot of research on diseases, cancer, nutrition and the human body. Combining all that I read and learned from natural healers such as Dr. Sebi. I've connected everything and have a blueprint to heal diseases.

DESTINY: Oh my goodness Seven, it's crazy you say that because I've been watching a lot of testimonies online. I have become infatuated with the thought of their being a natural cure.

KING: So the question is, what are you going to do with all the knowledge and wisdom you have acquired?

SEVEN: Do you remember me speaking on a writing project? Well, I've been writing this packet, a packet that consists of all essential information for the body, mind, and soul. With information inside that can assist you to healing your body naturally.

KING: I remember indeed. So you are going to finish it up and get it out there to the people?

SEVEN: Right. But the thing is, I'm not going to get it published. I'm leaning towards just passing it out to whomever my spirit tells me to. Or any one in need. For free.

DESTINY: Because if you get it published, you are getting the government involved, who is connected to the pharmaceutical companies. Especially if the packet makes a lot of noise.

KING: I'm feeling it. That is when you gain real power. When it's bigger than money. You are trying to enlighten and empower.

DESTINY: If you start freeing minds and helping people cure themselves, that means somebody is missing out on money.

KING: The big wigs who will send them people after you. They kill our hero's. That's why we don't really have any. So the next question to you is, basically, are you willing to die for the wellbeing of mankind?

SEVEN: That's a good question. Because over fifty holistic healers have mysteriously came up dead all in the same year. I don't have it all mapped out yet. But I'm definitely thinking of a master plan.

DESTINY: Fifty healer's in one year! And didn't Dr. Sebi just pass away shortly after he was retained by the police?

SEVEN: That is true. If I were to get the book published, I'm sure there are rules and regulations I would have to pass in order to put out this type of information. I would have to get it proved by this and that, while jumping through all the loops in order put out essential information that should be free.

KING: Ain't that something! They are wiping out healers and leaders man. Hell naw! That's why I can't work for them, or whoever they are. I'm not feeding that beast.

DESTINY: Evil. That is what you are up against. Not man, the evil spirit working through man to stop you.

KING: Yea man I dig that. I could use something like that too. Cause Lord knows I am not trying to see no doctor.

SEVEN: And there are many of us who feel the same way. I know it can bless people. Too many of us are deteriorating from a lack of knowledge. We're in some type of paralyzed state.

DESTINY: They say, we are what we eat.

● ● ●

KING: And what we think.

They carry on conversing while moving closer to the flashing lights of Vegas. Destiny would have King pull over so she could take pictures of the scenery. She took over the driving duties when King wanted a break. They all took turns on having a music session. After every hour they would switch DJ's. They joked around about who was DJ'ing the best. They would take turns driving passed the person in the car next to them on the road, and have to guess what type of person they were. From their mannerism, age, life style, habits, and whatever else came to their mind. They wanted to see if their people reading skills were on the same page. Or even in the same ballpark. While picking each other's brain, King receives a phone call.

KING: (Answer the phone) Hey mama sitas, I'm on my way... oh you miss me huh, well prove it by coming to see me tonight. I should make it in around one... that sounds like a plan. I'll call you when I get there.

DESTINY: Oh Lord, which one is this?

KING: Remy, that fine thick school teacher.

SEVEN: I see you, having them lined up waiting on you.

KING: Just a little something, nothing major.

DESTINY: Aww, so that is why he chose Las Vegas and the coast of Cali.

KING: (Grinning) Come on lil sister, you know how big bro do it. And it's that time. You know God say, "man is not meant to be alone." And plus you know I want to see Mayweather box before he retires. Fight weekend brings out the heavy traffic of people with money to spend. Why not lend it to a friend.

DESTINY: I'm not mad at ya, do your thang brother. I know you have a plan in that mind of yours.

SEVEN: So you say I can ask you anything right? And record the info and turn it in to a story with my own twist to it.

KING: In order to bring out the story, you simply need to know. So shoot my brother.

SEVEN: That's understood. So what's up with the ladies having a connection to your plan?

King was slumped down in his seat while blowing smoke out a crack of the window. The volume to the music was just right to play in the background. Destiny controls the wheel looking good as she wants to be. King takes one more drag of his black & mild before answering Seven's question.

KING: It's like this my brother. Through my eyes, how I see it, a lot of potentially great men who never reach their full potential allowed a woman to come in and shake up the design. That love can be a fool. Make us do some crazy things. That is how I ended up spending years of my life behind bars, all behind the power of love. But if I were to be focused, that wouldn't have happened in the first place. But we live and we learn. And what I've learned is that I will allow the right one to slow me down. I'm not on my game tough as I usually am when being involved. A woman slows me down. On top of that, there is a higher chance of getting caught and played. That's what happen to me. I thought I was coming to the rescue of my girl, but come to find out, her and someone who I thought was my friend set me up. I raised hell when I found out they planned the whole thing. I tore some shit up, slapped her around, beat the shit out of him to where he almost lost his life. And I was already on probation.

I got my mind right while being locked up. Learned from some old heads. Gathered up all the information, experienced, wisdom and understanding, that's when I decided that less was best. I became obsessed with wanting to execute this plan and create the life I want. But as we know, man is not meant to be alone. And with that being said, when Destiny and I go out and do our thing, I might meet a woman and show her a good time. I scope her out, see where her mind is at, and if she pass all my tests, I keep in contact with her. Showing her a good time and sexing her down real good will have me on her mind. The long distance and being consistent usually causes her to wonder about me. I make it to where we can be totally honest with each other. Well, besides her knowing what I do, but for the most part, honesty is the best policy. I might fly out and see her once every so often and become her fantasy. Then dip back home. She usually becomes at my mercy over time. And that is when I make a proposal to her.

I already know what you are thinking Seven, what does the proposal all consist of. Well, I'll tell you. I make her an offer that will be hard to refuse. Before I present it to her, I wanted to have four things establish in her mind. I'm not married, I'm playing with some cash, I'm honest and our sex is unforgettable. Those four things will have her undivided attention. I explain to her that she can do no wrong by me from being honest. That she is free to do whatever she likes. Free to see, date or screw anybody she likes, just be honest with me. So I will know what to do and not to do with her sexually. I'm not sure if you have noticed it by now, but I have a slight case of OCD. I'm not a big fan of germs or an unhealthy vagina. Because I most certainly plan on going down there. And when I do, I want it clean from being properly taken care of. Because if I catch something, she is going to wish she never met me.

So, it's basically like this, I come in town to visit, we might shop, we eat at great restaurants, or we might catch a movie. There has been some times she might run into a time of need and I give her the money. Besides that, just out the goodness of my heart I have paid some car notes, got her nails, feet, and hair done from just wanting to. For the moments we spend together I treat her as she is mine. I might randomly send her flowers at work, send her tickets to a concert or gift certificates to spa's on her birthday. All to keep her honesty valid and her body healthy. I expect two things. Honesty and a full STD screening results within three days before I see her. Far as the honesty, all she has to do is let me know if she is being sexually involved without protection so I'll know not to go down there, then, I will be able to decipher if I want to continue on being sexually active with her at all. Because I'm not just a hit it from the back type of guy. Naw, I need to explore that body and fulfill all my desires with her. So I need that thang right.

I do let it be known though, if she lies to me, it's not going to be good for her. I won't be a happy camper. Fortunately, that has not happened. Some have been honest and got into relationships, as they should. Some want more than what I have to offer, and so I have to lose contact with them. Better safe than sorry. And most find it easy to just go to doctor and get their health status, text it to me, and have it prepared when I see them. We get up every once in a while and have a good time. We don't bother each other, we have our own lives. I'm just a friend with great benefits. And just to make sure the STD results are valid, I have them take a picture of being in the health clinic. I need that proof. It's kind of hard for them to turn that down.

SEVEN: If I were in your shoes, it would make all the sense in the world to do so. So your lack of trust in people causes you to pay for their honesty and proof of not having a sexually transmitted disease? And so whenever you feel like going on a vacation, you have a lady lined up.

KING: That would be correct.

SEVEN: How many woman across the states do you have?

KING: Five. There is my white southern bell Bethany in Houston. My natural black goddess Jasmine from Atlanta. My Asian persuasion Roxanne from Cali. My sexy Latin I call Salena out in Miami. And there is Remy who happens to be mixed with black and Mexican in Vegas.

SEVEN: Must be nice boss man. I'm not trying to count your pockets, but you must spend a good deal of money on these women.

KING: Not really. These women are established and have their own. I give because they are giving me their body and time when I want it. I'm alone most of my days, so when I do travel I want to enjoy the whole experience of providing and loving. I sexually please them and they sexually please me, and we all do it in a safe and natural way. After that small amount of time, I'm fully focused and back on the job.

DESTINY: So have you ever ran into one and caught feelings. And if so, what did you do?

KING: Oh yea, a few times. I respected them enough to not want to waste their time. I wasn't ready like how they were. I would just be using them. Besides, the game I'm in, the closer they are, the more of a chance I could get them caught up in my dirt. These boys today will kidnap your girl and hold her for ransom. They will go after her kids. It's ruthless out here. How do I know, because I was that savage once upon a time.

SEVEN: If I had to take a guess, you are also low key seeing who could be your potential woman. That is after your mission is complete.

KING: This guy in the back seat is good. That's right on the mark. If I had to say right now, if I were ready to change my ways, the woman I'll see tonight is who I connect with the most.

DESTINY: Remy is my favorite of the ones I've met. I know she is a good girl who hopes for the day you take her on full time. I know you got it, but a sister who wants the best for her brother, I can't wait for the day you end up with your life partner. Slow down and be able to experience having a family.

KING: Me to sis. I'll be retired when that time comes. Then I would just be with my family, while the money from my business circulates from a far.

SEVEN: So that's the plan. Work the masterplan, start a business, and retire while enjoying your family.

KING: Sounds about right. It doesn't make sense to me as a father, to have to spend more time at a work place than my own kids. That don't sound right to me, nor does it feel right. My future kids need to see my face more than the school teacher's face. What kind of shit is that? There are too many of us men spending so much time away from home, the foundation of where it all starts. It's not supposed to be like this. That's like a disaster waiting to happen.

SEVEN: Modern day slavery.

DESTINY: That's for the birds.

It wasn't long before the three could spot out the Vegas lights from a distance. At one thirty AM is when they pulled up to the MGM Grand Hotel and Casino resort and checked in. After checking in, King handed Seven an envelope.

KING: I'll give you the rest once we get back to Texas. But for now, here is an advance. There is an extra $2,000 dollars for spending money for food or gambling. If you need more, let me know and I got you. After lunch we will go shopping for new clothes and shoes, and that's all on me.

Have you looking right out here. There is also a room key inside. All of our rooms are next to each other. Other than that, enjoy yourself man. You deserve it. Take it all in. It's your world.

Chapter **7**

LET THE GAMES BEGIN

The distant lover named Remy, joins the crew for lunch on a roof top restaurant. The table of four looks major without a major deal. Their energies combined caused for a magnet of attraction. They mingled while enjoying the weather, food, and scenery.

DESTINY: So how have you been doing miss teacher lady?

REMY: Girl, I've have been doing good, just out here living. Lot of working, but I can't complain about anything. Well, I could but it wouldn't do me no good. I know I've been missing your brother.

KING: (Leans over and puts his arm around Remy) Well I'm here now babe, and were gonna to live it up.

King notices Remy make a small noise of pain when hugging her. He also notices a mark on her neck once he leaned back in his seat. He takes a sip of his water and notices small bruises on her arm. He looked into Remy's eyes. He connects the marks to her mentioning how she could complain, but it wouldn't do her no good comment. Seven acted as if he wasn't aware and looked at all the people walking below.

DESTINY: Are you okay girl?

REMY: Yes, I'm good.

KING: How did you get those bruises?

REMY: ...I'm fine, just a little soar. No big deal.

There was an awkward silence at the table. King tells Remy to move back a part of her hair so he could view her neck. Destiny makes a sigh once she sees the marks on her neck. King doesn't change his look but remains calm.

KING: Who put those marks on you Remy?

REMY: Just some crazy guy named Ron who thinks he is untouchable.

(Destiny and King give each other that look that only they knew what it meant)

DESTINY: Well, you and me will discuss this individual later honey. We don't have to talk about this right now. In the mean time, let's go ball out.

• • •

King pats the top of Remy's hand and tells her that everything was going to be fine and not to worry. Everything is going to be taken care of. Seven could sense King's revengeful thoughts covered by his cool, calm, and collective demeanor.

After lunch, the four strolled the mall and shopped it up. Destiny nibbled on an ice cream cone while enjoying the company of Seven, while King charms Remy with his gentlemen hood like aura. King took Seven to the stores he would shop at for himself. He didn't allow Seven to shop as if he was on a budget. He made sure Seven got the top of the line quality gear, a few pairs of shoes and a nice watch. He wouldn't allow the pride of Seven to stop him from showing his appreciation. During the shopping spree is when Destiny mentally finagled her way into gathering all the information on Remy's abuser named Ron.

The night time arrives and lights were lit in Sin City. Lights, camera, and action for the tag team brother and sister. Both are suited and booted for the Mayweather fight at the MGM Grand Casino and Resort. The worldwide pay per view event brought out the fly guy in King who looked straight out of a GQ magazine. Destiny dazzles with her flawless skirt that brought out the curves in her coke bottle shaped body. Not that King was ever looking out for it, but out of respect, Seven would not allow King to catch him looking at Destiny's body. But when the coast was clear, he definitely got his peeks in.

Seven spends his evening at the swimming pool with his pen and pad. His mind raced with ideas while stretched out on a lawn chair. He munched down on a salad, veggie pizza, and sipped on a frozen rum pina colada. He watched the people around him have a good time while simultaneously writing his thoughts on paper. The surrounding vacationers wouldn't have guessed it, but he was having a great time by seeing them have a great time.

Back to the lights, camera, and action inside the arena. Destiny and King were rubbing elbows with celebrities left and right as they moved closer to their seats. The energy in the atmosphere was electric. Destiny transformed into character. She knew better to not judge a book by its cover when it came to the money. Most pocket books didn't match the outer appearance of the beholder. Most men she crossed paths with the most money were the less flashy ones. She was in the mindset of not turning down any ones phone numbers. She never knew who could lead her to the right person, event or after party. The more contacts, the more option's to explore.

The crowd cheers and boo's as Mayweather made his ring entrance. The cameras were rolling and the anticipation in the building was intense. Many people would mistake King for being a professional athlete. He used it to his advantage if the situation felt right. His eyes were on a prowl, looking for a bite to reel in. When both fighters made their way into the ring and the national anthem was sung, Destiny was already catching eyes from men in the crowd. The famous Michael Buffer made his signature, "LETS GET READY TO RUMBLE," and the crowd erupted. Once the fight started, the team enjoyed the experience.

Away from the fight scene, Seven made his way back up to his hotel room. A hot shower in the luxurious bathroom while he played music from his phone. He felt good putting on his new pair of shoes and clothes. Seven was the type that no matter what he was wearing, he made it look good. But when he decided to dress up he was one smooth debonair man. He left his room and stepped into the elevator. Inside the elevators were mirrors on all four sides. "Who is this person," he asked himself while checking out his sharp attire. A scent of cologne and a nice wrist watch to compliment his grown man style. He felt good while walking in the Vegas streets of hundreds of people. He found himself a spot to watch the fight.

Seven wasn't worried about anything back home at the moment, he was living in the now. Just the other day he was lying in a hospital bed, to now in Vegas enjoying the experience. Everything happened so fast and out of nowhere. He wondered if it was all orchestrated by God. He asked himself the question, "what brought me to cross paths with Destiny and King?" Right after asking himself the question, he looked up at the big screen and saw both of them sitting in the crowd right behind Jay Prince. An energy of inspiration and conformation eased his mind.

The fight was entertaining despite the masterful easy win for Mayweather. More money in the pocket for King and the night had just begun. After the crowd of thousands clear the buildings and scatter the Vegas streets is when Destiny takes a stroll alone. King follows her at a distance. They would eventually come together and game plan the next play. The night was still young and the drinks were kicking in for the people of the night. Calls and texts would be made and received throughout the night for plans and invites. They never knew what to expect on any given night. There was always one willing to be at Destiny's mercy or lead her to the money. The tag team make it back to the hotels parking garage and got into the Cadillac.

KING: While we wait to hear back from these new contacts, I figured we would go see about the man who put those marks on Remy.

DESTINY: Ron Cunningham. Ten minutes away from the hotel. According his twitter page, he will be at a spot called, The Grooves.

KING: So basically you are saying we should go teach his ass a lesson.

DESTINY: I most certainly am.

KING: My goodness I am in the presence of greatness.

DESTINY: I learned from the best. Now let's cut the chase big bro and go turn this scumbag into a sacrificial lamb. I've been itching to get next to this woman beater.

KING: You know what's crazy. Right now he is probably having a good time, throwing a few back and living it up, having a grand old time. But little does he know, his world is about to take an unexpected turn.

DESTINY: (Pulls the sun roof visor down and puts lipstick on in the mirror) Come to momma.

About 20 minutes later, a nice shiny Cadillac pulls in the parking lot with Texas license plates. Destiny leaves from the car first. Minutes later, King follows behind. Destiny turns into character as she walks past a line of people waiting to get inside the club. She turns heads from the men and women standing in line. Similar to a model walking the runaway, but more natural. It wouldn't matter if the greatest showman was in the building, Destiny was not waiting in line for no one. She pays a fee of skipping the line. Look out ahead, she's on her way to locating her prey. Her light steals the show as if she was making a ring entrance at a prize fight. She moved around the club ignoring the men that try and talk to her. She finally spots her reason in the VIP section. She surveys the area while thinking of a game plan.

It wasn't long before King spotted Destiny out inside the club. He kept his distance while watching her do her thing. With Destiny, it wasn't if she caught her prey, it was when she caught him. Destiny walks up to the bouncer standing in front of the VIP entrance. He asks if her name was on the list, and she replies yes, although she knew it wasn't. Before he begins to read off the list, she fixes his collar while looking him in his eyes.

DESTINY: There you go.

BOUNCER: (Appreciating the fact that she didn't need her space) Thank you Miss Lady.

DESTINY: I got you.

BOUNCER: I don't see your name on the list ma'am. Maybe they forgot to add you.

DESTINY: (Turns around in a circle so the bouncer could see what she was working with) They forgot about me. Well, that's just messed up. He had me drive all the way out here and forgot to put my name on the list.

BOUNCER: Yea they definitely left the wrong one out. Because, by the looks of it, there has to be a mistake.

DESTINY: No that's okay. They got your girl all the way faded if they think I'm going to be begging to get in a VIP. I'll go buy me a section babe. But you can do something for me.

BOUNCER: Oh I got you, talk to me.

DESTINY: (Moves a little closer to him while looking in his eyes) You see that man over there wearing the blazer jacket?

BOUNCER: Yeah I see him.

DESTINY: Can you tell him that I want to buy him a drink. Can you do that for me big daddy?

BOUNCER: Yea I got you.

Destiny acts as if she can smell his cologne. She moves her nose near his neck and guesses what cologne he is wearing. Little did he know, Destiny was reading off names on his VIP list.

DESTINY: That is either some Ralph Lauren cologne, or just some good smelling deodorant that goes good with your pours. Either way I love a good smelling man.

BOUNCER: (Laughing from recognizing her flirtatious sense of humor) Naw, just a good old few swipes of deodorant.

DESTINY: Okay, well I guess I'll head home after I have me a drink.

BOUNCER: Wait, don't you want me to go check with the guy. There has to be a mistake here.

DESTINY: I mean obviously there has to be a mistake. I'm looking at some of my friends right now. There is Steve and Brandon right there, and I know Saundra is back there somewhere.

BOUNCER: (He looks at his list and notices the names she called off where on the VIP list) Yea, they are in here. Yea, I don't know how happen but... I tell you what.

DESTINY: (Acts as if she was waving at someone behind the him in VIP) What is that big daddy, talk to me.

BOUNCER: Yea, I guess I'll go ahead and let you in. Sorry about the little mix up. That happens time to time.

DESTINY: (She leans over and gives him a hug) Oh you are just a breath of fresh air, and a cuddling bear, oh I like.

BOUNCER: Alright now, come back and talk to me.

DESTINY: Will see Pappi.

King found him a spot at the bar and watched at a distance. Once she spotted him at the bar is when she carried on by working her magic. Ron was standing with two other guys. She stood directly in front of him about ten yards away. She just stood there and stared at him until he noticed her. Once he spotted Destiny out, he double takes to make sure his eyes were not deceiving him. She didn't budge at all, standing right there looking directly into Ron's eyes. He looked behind him to see if she was looking at someone else so he stares back. The DJ mixed in another song and Destiny starts dancing seductively to the music while the flashing lights glowed off her melanated skin. She mentally pictures where his car keys could be located in his pockets. Ron stands and watches her groove. Once she sees him smiling back is when she signaled her finger for him to come closer. He walks over to her and stands in front of her.

DESTINY: What took you so long? I been waiting for you to come talk to me.

RON: Oh, you have?

DESTINY: We passed by each other when you first walked in and I been watching you ever since.

RON: I'm just now seeing you. Who are you here with?

DESTINY: It's just me handsome.

RON: What's your name?

DESTINY: Heaven, and yours?

RON: Heaven, you sure are. My name is Ron. Where are you from?

DESTINY: Texas. I'm on a work vacation.

RON: So have you enjoyed yourself?

DESTINY: Not yet. I've been working the whole time. So I decided to step out tonight and let loose before I catch my flight back to Texas in the morning.

RON: Let loose huh?

DESTINY: It's been so long since I went out drinking and talked to a cute guy.

The DJ mixes in another song and Destiny starts to slow dance in front of him. She locked eyes with Ron while grooving close to him. She turns and faces the other direction while leaning her body up against his.

A personal show for Ron before the two start to vibe and mingle amongst themselves.

DESTINY: I'm going to the bar Pappi, what do you want to drink?

RON: You are going to buy me a drink?

DESTINY: What, a boss lady can't buy you a drink?

RON: No, it just never happens. But sure, I'll have a Blue Moon.

DESTINY: Sure thing, I'm going to the ladies room first and I'll be back with your drink.

RON: Alright, I'll be here, you come back now.

DESTINY: Oh don't you worry, I shall return.

She leaves his side and makes eye contact with King on the way out of VIP. They met up at the end of bar and walked towards the front entrance. King acted as if he was drunk when approaching the front entrance. Destiny put one arm around her brother to help him from staggering. She informs the bouncer that she called an Uber driver so her friend could get home safe and would return back. The bouncer gave the okay and watched them leave the building.

Once both were out of sight of the bouncers view, Destiny pulled out the car keys she picked pocket from Ron. She managed to slip them out of the side pocket of his blazer jacket when dancing close to him. She signals the alarm so they could hear where his car was located in the parking lot. King snapped out his act of being drunk before spotting the car at a distance.

From back inside the club, Ron glances around to see if he could spot out Destiny. She was already in his mind. It wasn't long before he spots her making her way out from around the bar with a Blue Moon in her hand. She gives him an embrasive look with her arm out wanting a hug. Soon as Ron leaned in to hug her is when she hugs him back and remains connected for a moment. In the mist of hugging, she slipped his keys back in the side pocket of his blazer jacket. Right as she released the keys in his pocket, she pulled away and says, "I'm sorry, I get a little extra lovey dovey when I drink. Hope it's not too much for you." Ron doesn't mind having his ego stroked at all. He walks her over towards some of his buddies and introduces her. They begin to mingle before Ron eventually pulls Destiny aside and they both have a seat.

RON: So, who are you?

DESTINY: Wait a minute, before we carry on, tell me now, are you like a lot these fake females out here, or a real woman who knows what she wants?

RON: There ain't nothing like the real thang babe, that's what Marvin said, and that is my kind of speed. Now, are you going to answer my question?

DESTINY: I told you, my name is Heaven and I've been sent to bless you.

Ron: And how can you bless me?

DESTINY: I can show you better than I can tell you.

RON: Who are you here with?

DESTINY: I'm a lone female wolf tonight.

RON: Heaven sent huh? Yeah I hear you talking. Sounds almost too good to be true. If you are a straight shooter like you claim, what is it that you are looking for?

DESTINY: I'm on a work vacation. I've done the work part, but not the vacation part. I'm in Vegas and I've yet to have fun, and I'm ready to have some. If I were to be in your shoes, I would be cautious of me from my strong approach. But the truth is, I'm always a good girl, but I don't want to be tonight. I'm a workaholic who hasn't been laid in forever. I'm a picky chooser, but when I first saw you, I just felt something. So if I scare you, I understand. But if you are down to just live life tonight and make each other feel good, wuz up. I was thinking we can go to my hotel room and you put me to sleep. And when I wake up in the morning I'll be on my way back home. Or, if that is too much for you, we can just go hang out and vibe.

RON: (Ron grabs her hand and holds it in the air so he could spin her around in a circle) How can a man pass this once in a life time opportunity up?

DESTINY: But then again I don't know, who is to say I won't have you falling in love after one night.

● ● ●

RON: Oh you want to find out what O Ronnie Ron is about. Okay, well tonight must be both of our lucky night.

DESTINY: (Moves in closer to his face and stares into his eyes) Take me somewhere.

RON: Right now?

DESTINY: We can take the party to my room. Or to your place, or we ditch this place and go kiss on each other in the car like we are young again.

RON: You naughty woman you.

DESTINY: I understand if I intimidate you, I attend to have that effect on men.

RON: Oh no babe you met your match tonight. And I'm going to be the one to bless you once it's all said and done.

DESTINY: Oh I have that feeling daddy, but only thing is, you still talking.

RON: Are you calling my bluff?

DESTINY: And I'm pulling yo card. Talk about it or be about it.

RON: Damn. Are all Texas girls like you?

DESTINY: There is only one of these that you will find. Consider this a night you will never forget.

RON: You talk a good game, but I got something for that. Let's ride out. Did you drive?

DESTINY: No I took a taxi.

RON: You can ride with me.

DESTINY: Oh I'm a ride alright.

Ron makes up a story of why he was leaving the party early. Destiny sends King a text while they both leave the club together. Ron sees the readiness in her eyes while walking to the car. He moves in closer and puts his arm around her waist. She moves away from him by walking a few steps ahead just so he could see her booty move. She turns her head back while still walking forward and gives him a seductive look. His desire for her rises while watching her move from behind. He catches up with her and guides her to his car. She made sure to have his eyes on her before he opens the passenger door, speaking meaningless nothings in his ear. He walks around the front of the car and gets into the driver seat. Ron leans over and tries to kiss Destiny but she shields away from him by saying, "let's save it all for the hotel room." He asks what hotel they were going to and she gives him the wrong name. Out of nowhere King rises up from the backseat and points a gun at the back of Ron's head.

KING: Move and I'll send a bullet to your brain!

RON: (Scared and shook while raising his hands) DON'T SHOOT!

● ● ●

KING: Relax, if you cooperate you will go home tonight safe in all one piece.

RON: (Looks at Destiny) You set me up bitch!

Destiny quickly grabs ahold of his testicles and squeezed. Ron jerked into a paralyzed freeze and lets out a squeal of pain. While at her mercy, she tells Ron to give up his cell phone and wallet while King presses the barrel of a silencer on a 22 handgun. In a calm manner King addresses Ron, "that was your one and only pass, the next time you decide to get fly, I'm going to cripple you for life. Do I make myself clear?" Ron squeals out a painful yes, before Destiny releases her grip on his testicles. He lets out a sigh of relief while clutching his crotch. King sits back in his seat while still holding the gun at the back of Ron's head. "Why me man," Ron cries out. "You have been chosen, consider us to be your karma," King replies. Once Destiny has both his cell phone and wallet is when she gets out of the car and gets into the backseat.

KING: Here is the deal. Before I give you two options, I'll tell you what brings me here. There is a woman by the name of Remy you put your hands on. And it is my duty to protect her.

RON: I'm sorry. I'll never see her again.

KING: Here are your two options. One, Remy has five marks on her body that were caused by you. I counted while making love to her. Which means I take a finger for every mark. And have you drive me to your home and I rob you blind.

• • •

RON: (In a helpless manner) Oh my God! Please no, please!

KING: Partner in crime, what is the name of this weak man?

DESTINY: (Holds up his driver's license while taking a picture of it with her personal phone) Looks like we have, Ron here.

KING: Ron. Don't worry Ron, because I've been told, when you call on that name God, there is hope. Which brings me to your option number two. You donate to our charity and go home tonight with only your feelings hurt.

RON: Option two! I have money, we can go to the ATM machine right now.

KING: Naw Ronnie, bank is closed at this time of night. You have to think of all the money that would add up to missing fingers, surgery, and precious valuables in your home.

DESTINY: Don't forget about this car we're in, a chop shop cold break this sexy thing down and pay out some real cash.

KING: You sho right. But you know what, if he cooperates, we could work out a reasonable deal.

RON: Option two it is, what do I need to do?

KING: Is that your final answer?

RON: Yes, for crying out loud!

KING: Lower your voice. Tha hell is wrong with you, put this business transaction on pause and beat your ass.. Is that how you conduct business? Now that we have a deal, it is only wise of me to protect myself. Because who is to say you won't go to the police and turn us in. Give details to a sketch artist, or have someone to come after Remy. There will be consequences. Tell us a little more about that my partner in crime.

DESTINY: We have a Ron who lives at address, 206 Pathway Drive, Las Vegas Nevada. Two little daughters, and aww their sooo cute, who live with the baby mama. I have the numbers here. I will call her, and you will apologize it's late, but you need her address now so you can send the girls a surprise. I will have you on speaker phone, if you try anything funny, the deal is off and you will suffer the consequences. So straighten up and quit crying.

The phone rings while Ron clears his voice. The baby momma answers the phone out of her sleep and Ron does as he is told. She tells him the address while Destiny collects the data.

KING: Now Ron, I know where you live. I know where your kids live. I have your driver's license and credit card information that will be sent by text to a number of someone close by. And if anything were to happen to us, or you were to contact the police, the person will come and kidnap your children if he can't find you. But

I am pretty sure he will find you. That's what he is trained to do. But if we never hear from you again, you will never see us again. If you manage to move to another location and rat us out later, my client has retrieved the contact numbers to your parents, relatives, and friends. We will take out people just to get to you. Do you understand? (King didn't have a side client, but he wanted Ron to believe that he did)

RON: Yes, I understand.

KING: Well, let's get this transaction started shall we.

RON: How about ten thousand.

KING: You know what Ron, I have even a better idea. How about you tell her the password to your bank account on your phone.

DESTINY: I'm ready when you are, I already have the screen up.

RON: (Putting his head on the steering wheel) aww shit man. This is a nightmare.

KING: I'll show you a real nightmare if you don't stop playing around. Let's get to it before I change my mind and take your money, yo car and five fingers.

RON: Ok! Alright.

Destiny holds the phone up towards Ron to where all he had to do is type his password on the screen. Ron regretfully types in his password and the amount in his account displays on the screen. Ron wore a defeated look. Destiny looks at the displayed number on the phone and leans back in the seat. She looks at King and he stares back at her in a brief moment of silence. She lifts the phone up to King so he could see the amount. He witnesses the amount, looks back at Destiny and they both just smiled at each other.

KING: You thinking what I'm thinking?

DESTINY: Maybe, what you thinking?

KING: It's time for church. Followed up by receiving a generous offering from brother Ron.

DESTINY: God loves a cheerful giver. But first things first. Since the bank is closed they have invented this wonderful thing called, money transfer. Where you can send large sums of money by phone in the matter of seconds. Technology, technology.

KING: It's a fool ain't it.

RON: (Trying to hold back tears) This is messed up man.

DESTINY: Correction, what's messed up is you putting your hands on a woman. You are lucky my partner is giving you options, because if it was up to me, I would take your money, car, and leave you crippled while tattooing the word coward on your forehead.

KING: Yea, I second that, she would indeed. Maybe I'm getting soft. But hey, you know what Ron, I haven't had to pistol whip you yet. And you have been cooperating, so I'm going to cut you a break. I'm not going to break the bank, but I am going to take a lump sum. But don't worry, it's going to a good cause. So wipe those tears away and hold your head up for being a part of a good cause. You are a good cowardly man Ron.

DESTINY: With some weak ass game.

KING: He can't help it, he's just doing what's in him.

DESTINY: Let's get to this business transaction. I see you already have your account set up to be able to send large amounts of money. So I'm going to hand you your phone back and give you the information to this anonymous account to send the money to.

KING: This is all happening so smoothly like it was all meant to be.

DESTINY: Look at God.

KING: Won't he do it!

DESTINY: (Hands Ron the phone to make the transaction) Now, while you be a blessing to our charity, let's have church.

RON: What's the amount?

DESTINY: I already entered the amount. Just add the rest of the information it asks and hit send.

RON: (Looks at the amount and shakes his head in disgust)

DESTINY: Since the amount is so large your about to get a call any second from your bank to make sure you authorized the transaction.

KING: (Lowered his gun) You see Ron, even with what you will be giving away, you still are well off financially. I know men who would love to be in your shoes by having plenty of money, an expensive car, and living in a high rise. But you have lost sight by taking all that you have for granted, due to selfishness and thinking you are above the law. Thinking you can walk around and beat on women. You let all that money get to your mind. You could lose all that you have behind one moment of a lack of self- control. Luckily you caught a break and will only lose half. But this here will cause you to check your pride and ego, which is entirely out weighing your heart. Life check homie, time to re-evaluate yourself and make the proper changes that won't hurt others. Partner do you have anything?

DESTINY: It makes me sick how you handle us women. Like we're some piece of meat or a punching bag. No sir, we are the mother of us all. None of us would be here if it wasn't for the woman. Ask yourself the question, would you want a man like you to date your daughters when they are older? That's something to think about.

Ron's phone rings. He answers to hear the voice of a 24 hour representative of his bank. King points the 22 to the back of his head. Ron answers a couple of questions to confirm the transaction and hangs up.

● ● ●

KING: And to bring this message to a close. Look on the bright side Ron, you still have your health, career, your daughters, wellbeing, possessions, and unharmed. You just lost something that really carries no value. Take the money away, then who are you? Not so big after all huh, over there crying. But tonight that changes, and you have an opportunity to wake up and realize what's important. You just lost out on some money, but you can bounce back. Don't think of this as a loss, think of it as you taking a business hit. And that hit brought about a valuable life lesson.

A sound alerted Destiny's phone that read, transaction complete. She checks the anonymous account to confirm the money was there. King looks at Ron through the rear view mirror and says, "let this be the last we hear from each other. Pleasure doing business with you. Both King and Destiny get out of the car at the same time. Ron watched both vanish off while he cried in his car. The brother and sister walked calm and collective to the Cadillac and drove off. Once they pulled away from the parking lot they both looked at each other and started shouting in celebration. While driving away from the clubs parking lot, there was a big strobe light that waved into the sky to bring attention to their clubs establishment.

From looking outside his window of his near roof top hotel room, Seven can see the moving strobe light. He follows the light weave in and out of the dark sky and continues to write. Once King and Destiny made it back to the hotel is when they carry on to their separate room. Soon as King walked into his room, their laid a naked Remy awaiting him. He walks over to the edge of the bed and lives in the moment. Glass house view, eye level with sky scrapers, while looking at the masterful work of God's creation laying there. She awakes after hearing him remove his clothes. Love making in a luxury suite, high above ground with neon lights surrounding down below.

When Destiny walks into her room, Seven could hear that she made it back. She takes all her clothes off and lays in the bed. She puts a pillow in between her legs while looking out the glass house window that shows the city. Seven puts his pen down and sits at the edge of the bed while looking in the direction of Destiny's room. At the same time, they both quietly walk over to the wall that separates each other's room. They both gently place their ear up to the wall. They both carefully listen for any sounds that could enhance their imagination. Little did they know, they both stood in the same spot in separate rooms, doing the same exact thing. Only a wall divided them from standing within a foot apart.

Chapter

8

THE COAST OF CALI

The trio eat brunch together while sharing their stories of the night before. Destiny insists that their work in Vegas is done and now ready to go visit her favorite place on Cali coast. The plan sounded good to King and Seven so after eating they packed up and hit the road. All three souls are alive and full of life while cruising down highway 15. The sun roof was open, the music was jamming, and expectations were high.

DESTINY: I can't wait Seven, you are going to love this place. It's my favorite of them all.

SEVEN: What do you love about this place Destiny?

DESTINY: I love how it makes me feel. It's on the beach, but it's kind of ducked off about a mile away from the area where the people are. It's like a hidden heaven. A home away from home. The Cali weather is just so wonderful, and the sound of the ocean is therapeutic. I went to school with a friend of mine and her husband owns the beech house where we will be staying. It's nice, kind of secluded, great scenery, and location. The beech house is perfect for a couple. I can see you writing on the balcony or on the beach.

SEVEN: That sounds lovely. How often do you visit this place?

DESTINY: Once a year, sometimes two. I like to go on 4th of July and stay for a week. My friend and her husband live right outside LA. This is their getaway spot. They always said I can rent it out whenever I like.

KING: Yea she's ready to leave her brother by my lonesome.

DESTINY: Boy please, you know I'll be flying to where ever you are on the regular. You need to come live out here while you playing. It's time to retire and start a family.

SEVEN: What if you are already there, but it's just being accustomed to the lifestyle makes it harder to leave?

KING: Maybe. It's a rush like no other, to have nothing, to use your mind and make a move that covers all your expenses for a year. To not have to work or answer nobody. That fast money is addictive man.

DESTINY: I agree, it's so easy once it comes natural. Beats sitting in traffic, punching in a clock, and slaving.

SEVEN: Easy, how so?

DESTINY: I can show you better than I can tell you.

KING: (Looks at Destiny and she looks back) You thinking what I'm thinking?

DESTINY: Maybe, what are you thinking?

KING: It's almost time to get gas and there is a station coming up less than ten miles.

The black Cadillac pulls into a busy gas station and parks at a pump. King tells Seven to sit tight and watch Destiny work. He gets out of the car first and walks into the store to pay for gas. Destiny informs Seven to lean back in his seat so it will look as if shes alone. The tinted windows were enough shade to have Seven go unnoticed. Destiny gets out of the car and takes the window cleaner brush in between gas pumps and begins wiping the window down on all four sides. It only took a couple of minutes for a man to spot her at a distance. The young man pulls his car up to the gas pump on the opposite side of the Cadillac. When Destiny begins to pump gas is when she makes eyes contact with the intrigued man who looks to be in his mid -twenties. She gives him a flirtatious look to draw him in.

YOUNG MAN NAMED MIKE: Hey pretty lady.

DESTINY: Hey handsome.

MIKE: You sure are looking mighty nice.

DESTINY: (Smiling, but not responding back)

MIKE: (His back turned away from his car from checking out Destiny) Are you from around here?

DESTINY: (Starts to clean the window slightly leant over) No, but I'll be in town for a few days.

MIKE: Can I get your number and call you sometime. Sure would like to talk to you.

DESTINY: (She stops and gives him a look as if she isn't sure) I like your confidence.

MIKE: There is more to me.

DESTINY: (Walks up to the man and looked in his eyes) Alright. You ready?

MIKE: (He pulls out his cell phone out and types in her number) What is your name?

DESTINY: Nefertiti.

MIKE: My name is Mike.

DESTINY: Nice to meet you Mike.

She turns around while still making eye contact and gets into the car. Mike smiles while saving her number in his phone. He gets into the driver's seat and closes the door. King was sitting in the back seat with his 22 hand gun pointed at Mike.

KING: Don't move or I end your life.

MIKE: (Drops his phone when throwing his hands in the air)

KING: Relax, put your hands down and don't look at me. If you listen to me, I won't hurt you and you'll be on your merry way.

MIKE: Okay, I'll listen, don't shoot, I have kids.

KING: (Looks over at Destiny and she shakes her head no) Oh is that right. How many kids do you have?

Mike: Two boys.

KING: Are you involved in their lives?

MIKE: Yes I am, they're everything to me.

KING: Are you still with their mother?

MIKE: Yes.

KING: I see. So what's the deal with you trying to get with the woman in the Cadillac?

MIKE: I just thought she was fine as hell and wanted to see what's up.

KING: Do you and your woman love each other.

MIKE: Yes, she gets on my damn nerves.

KING: Look at me through the rear view mirror... I'm going to cut you a break today because I have a feeling you are a good guy who just out here being a young man. Otherwise, if you would have told me that you are not involved in your kid's life, today would have been a bad day for you. I would have took your car, have you empty your bank account, and knocked your ass out if you were to give me any problems in the process. You see, I was that child who didn't have the father and that's all I really wanted. Your taking what you have for granted. You were willing to throw away what you have, because you may think the grass is greener on the other side. You saw a fine woman and just had to see what's up. Little do you know, that woman could have got you caught up and you could have lost the woman who does love you. Over what? Because your selfish, and you are not thinking. You already know, all hell will break loose if she finds out about this new number in your phone. You think she hasn't evaluated that phone while you were sleep or in the shower? Maybe not. That can break you two apart and there you have it, two more black boys growing up without their father living in the same household. All because your weak behind a little piece of ass. Man there ain't shit out here. Don't take that love you have at home for granted. It's not all about you, it's bigger than you once you have kids. I don't know your situation, but if you love each other, try cherishing your woman, and watch how her getting on your nerves changes.

King gets out the car and stands there for a moment. He pulls his shades from the collar of his shirt and puts them on. He walks over to the Cadillac and drives off. Seven witnessed the whole thing.

SEVEN: (Looking at the brother and sister in disbelief) It's that easy. Just like that huh?

DESTINY: When dealing with so many lustful spirits and a lack of loyalty by a man, it's just that easy.

SEVEN: You could have took his money and his car. Well, did you get anything from him?

KING: Just his attention. Left him with a message.

DESTINY: Just a little practice.

KING: Remember, we only hit up people who have it coming to them or need a little wake up call.

SEVEN: That was crazy! It's like you two know what the other one is thinking. You two are some smooth operators.

King smoked his black & mild cigar and was cool as a fan. He showed no signs of worry, fear or doubt after he just pulled out a gun on someone. Seven knew King had the juice. He was a cold-blooded smooth criminal, who just happens to have a big heart. Destiny sat without a care in the world, as if she didn't just easily use her power to get what she wanted on a man. She glances back at Seven in the back seat and gives him a little smile. All Seven could do was smile back and take it all in. The young humble author was in a calm shock from just witnessing a real live scene in a movie.

They cruised the highway and conversed all the way until reaching their destination. They wasted no time hitting the beach. People on a boat passing by waved at the three sitting on the shore. The beech house was about thirty yards behind where they sat. Destiny dug her toes in the sand. Seven wrote in his note pad while King sat looking ahead with his elbows rested on his bent knees.

KING: Seven, I bet you could write for hours out here.

SEVEN: I believe so too my brother. Destiny was right, I love it out here.

DESTINY: What are you thinking over there?

SEVEN: Why me? Why allow me to come along and be a part of this experience. It all feels real. That is all I've really been searching for.

KING: To answer your question, ever since you came into the picture, I been thinking about God a lot. How we all came together, it had to been orchestrated by a higher power. There has always been this void in my life. I believe there is a God, I just haven't been cool with God. I don't understand why my life has been full of strife sorrow. I have anger in my heart and I can't seem to remove it. You two are the only pure hearts that I know. I already feel like I can do anything, but ever since you came around, I feel like I can walk on that water. That has to be God. I know the bible very well, I've read it a couple times and studied many scriptures, but my faith hasn't been there. You give having faith a chance.

DESTINY: You are a breath of fresh air. Seems like you were chosen to come reach us, and us to reach you.

SEVEN: (Looks out into the ocean. Then looks at the chill bumps on his arms) You two are giving me life. My eyes have opened even more. Much love and respect.

Destiny tells the boys to scoot in closer so she can take a picture. They move in closer and she holds the phone out and snaps a picture. The ocean water arises up further on to the shore, surrounding the three. King jumped to his feet, "come walk on this water with me," and started running into the ocean water. Seven and Destiny followed behind. The birds of the air sang while the clouds painted the blue sky. A surfer rode a wave not far from the crew. King dives into a current wave that pushed him closer to the shore. Seven tasted the ocean water for the first time. There was a couple walking in the sand while holding hands. Destiny wiped the water from her face and stood in the water watching the couple pass by.

The two men quietly creeped from behind, King lifted one foot of Destiny and Seven lifted the other foot close to the water's surface. Destiny went up in the air with her hands stretched out towards the sky. She tilted her head back while crying out a quick prayer in her mind, "God have grace and mercy on my soul," before they tossed her in the air. Once she lands under water, she stays a moment before coming back up for air. She rises out the water as if she had been baptized. The water slicks her hair back. Her smile was bright as the sun. "Oh it's like that huh, okay," and swims towards the boys who were in laughter. She splashes water in their direction. After their brief swim, they sat at shore and ate fruit and sipped wine. No one spoke for twenty minutes until King speaks.

KING: What is it Seven, how do you do it? How do you move so sinlessly? So graceful in a world full of chaos. Not having your family or your parents like us. How did you manage to become pure? What is the key, you can see what it did to me. I don't know what it's like to be happy.. I'm a savage.

SEVEN: I would have to say for me, mastering the two main commandments. Everything else seems to fall in place. Love God with all my heart while putting God first. And love my neighbors as myself. The common denominator of the two commandments is the key word, love. Love drives out fear and hate. What you put out, will come back. The only thing with that is, why haven't we experienced so much of that love to come back in return? Or, how can we know how to love when being deprived of it for so long? How can one know how to love, when they haven't learned how to love? Maybe we have been set apart for a task designed by God, and within that task, it isn't meant for us to experience so much love at this point of our lives. I haven't got that far yet. I don't think you are a savage, I think you are just a different kind of disciple. If a man like you were to give his life to God, it would be a powerful thing. Ground shaking, spell breaking, and history making.

DESTINY: An unstoppable force that could bring about change.

It hits home with King, although he doesn't show it on the outside. He put his shades on and stares out into the ocean to masks his emotions. No more words were spoken by King. Seven wasn't sure if he offended King, but was okay if he did, so the blood would be off his hands. Destiny lays back and stares at the sky and feeling the sand in her hands. Seven left all his worries back home and chose to live in the present. While caught in the moment, he felt something crawling on his foot. Seven wiped the beetle off and watched it crawl towards Destiny.

King and Destiny's thoughts quieted them down the rest of the evening. Seven sat on the balcony and watched the world in front of him. The tag team duo got dressed to impress and set out to see what fish they could fry. You could feel a tension in the car with the brother and sister when driving to the exclusive night club. A straight faced, marvelously dressed to impress Destiny rode in silence. King was sharp as a blade but didn't have total tunnel vision. He parks the car and turns the engine off. Before Destiny gets out of the car, she puts on a wig and adjusts it in the mirror. She looks at King while putting her hand over his hand.

DESTINY: I hate knowing my big brother doesn't know what it feels like to be happy. Maybe you never will until you fill that void. Only you know what that is my brother.

She gets out of the car and walks towards the front entrance. King watches for a moment and follows her move. Once he was inside the club amongst the crowd, he sees himself in the mirror on the wall. He stood there in the middle of the dancing crowd and watched himself in a daze. He snaps out of it after being bumped into by a woman who looks him up and down like he was a tall piece of candy. She dances in front of King before he spots out Destiny in the corner of his eye. He immediately follows her trail, leaving the woman left hanging. He finds a spot to keep an eye on her. He found himself disgusted by seeing his sister operate. He knew she didn't feel like working tonight. His thoughts have altered over the last hours. He doesn't care to see all these men in his sister's face.

Destiny dazzles as usual. She was a master at putting her feelings aside, and doing what she came to do. And that was taking care of business. A shark bit her bait and fell into their trap. Destiny texts King the play and gave the signal when to leave. She gave him enough time to go have the car started up and prepared to follow. Minutes later he watches his sister get into the car with a stranger. King was in conviction while following the car with his sister inside. He followed them into the motel parking lot where he could see the room from the outside. He watched how the man put his arm around Destiny as they walked up the stairs to the second floor. He could sense how she was faking it. After seeing her enter the room is when his peace became disrupted with a bad feeling.

Once inside the hotel room, Destiny always texts a thumbs up to let King know she felt comfortable. The signal on her phone was low to where she couldn't make a text. She hears all the locks on the door being locked behind her. She moves to a different spot in the room to see if she could catch a good signal. She holds the phone up in the air but no luck. When she raises her arm down and turns around, the man named Lloyd, was standing right in front of her. Lloyd was a thorough man who didn't have much of a personality. An uncomfortable charm with little to say.

DESTINY: Whoa! You snuck up quick.

LlOYD: Hopefully I didn't scare you.

DESTINY: No your fine, I just can't seem to catch a signal is this room.

LlOYD: No need for a phone right now, stay awhile. You say your name is Gloria right?

DESTINY: Yes

LlOYD: Right. Gloria, short for glorious. That, I thought you would be before knowing a little bit about you. I saw potential in those eyes. I guess looks can be deceiving, because you are a home wrecker. Willing to run off with a married man to go have sex in hotels. You make me sick, but my flesh desires you, and my soul needs you. I say that I am married, but really I'm not any more. My wife died over a two years ago. I've tried to sleep with women, I get to this point and just don't feel it. I'm still not ready. I'm not going to waste your time. I'll pay you if you just stay and talk to me. Maybe even letting me hold you in the bed.

● ● ●

DESTINY: (Holds back tears but plays it off well) Sure, we can do that, you can hold me, just let me go to the bathroom first and I'll be back.

Lloyd watches her closely walk to the bathroom. She walks in and closes the door behind her. She looks in the mirror and stops herself from crying. She checks her phone and still has no signal. She knew King was thinking all kinds of thoughts right now. Too much is going on in her mind. She feels scared and lost at the time. While trying to get herself mentally together, she sees that Lloyd has turned off all the lights outside the bathroom. A sick feeling came over her from not wanting to be there. She even thought about just running out of the room to her brother.

A moment later, she then feels the presence of Lloyd standing outside the bathroom door. Lloyd put his ear to the door. He lightly pressed the palm of his hand up against the door and begins to massage the door. She could hear him breathing. He then calls Destiny by name of his deceased wife named Angela... "Angela, are you okay in there sweetheart?" Destiny put her hand over her mouth in fear, while tears filled her eyes. "Angela... Angela... come out of there." "I will be out in a second" she replies. Silence and darkness was the feel outside the bathroom door. She wipes her face and checks her phone. Still no signal. She looks in the mirror and doesn't see the woman she wants to be, but now wasn't the time. She gathers herself by taking a couple of deep breaths. Soon as she opens the bathroom door, Lloyd was standing there.

DESTINY: (Jumped from being scared) My goodness Lloyd, you scared me!

LLOYD: Do I make you nervous?

DESTINY: No, your fine. I'm just feeling light headed. I'm not feeling well. I think I need to go.

LLOYD: (Facial expression changed) So you are ready to leave me? Just like how Angela left me.

DESTINY: I'm sorry, I just need to go and get some rest. I think I had too much to drink.

LLOYD: That's odd... I don't remember seeing you having a drink tonight.

Lloyd stands in front of the door blocking the entrance way. He massages his forehead with one hand and waves his finger no with the other.

LLOYD: You see, women like you need to be taught a lesson for being bad. Willing to sleep with a married man, then plays with my emotions, to now trying to leave me. (A forced laugh while staring into her eyes) What did I do? TELL ME! WHERE DID I GO WRONG THIS TIME?

Destiny tries to walk past him but he grabs her arm aggressively and pulls her close. Before she could scream, he put his hand over her mouth and tells her to be quiet. Destiny knees him between the legs. Lloyd lets out a painful grunt. He grabs on to Destiny so she could fall to the ground with him. Two shots were fired at the front door, followed by a loud bang from the door being kicked in. King walks inside with his gun pointed at Lloyd who was folded up in pain. King walks over and lifts Destiny up from the ground. She embraced her brother before they both ran out of the hotel room. People began stepping outside their hotel rooms from hearing all the loud ruckus. King and Destiny raced through the parking lot and got inside the Cadillac and burned off before allowing more witnesses to identify their car.

KING: Are you okay, did he hurt you?

DESTINY: I don't want to do this anymore!

KING: No more, were done okay. No more of this.

DESTINY: That's two close calls, those are signs.

KING: I'm ready to give my life to God.

DESTINY: (Forgets what just happened and looks at king) What did you say?

KING: I'm tired of running. That's the only thing I haven't tried. Maybe it's the void I have been missing. I always believed, but never accepted Jesus as my lord and savior. Not the white washed Jesus, but the actual son of God. I can't keep going on without at least giving it a shot. I think now is the time before it gets too late.

(Ten miles away, Seven was sitting on the beach while on the phone with his girlfriend)

GIRLFRIEND: A surprise visit to Vegas and Cali?

SEVEN: It's more like a business trip. I'm getting so much work done.

GIRLFRIEND: You sure you're not out there with a woman?

SEVEN: No. It sounds odd, but you do not have anything to worry about. This is all good news, I'll explain everything when I get back.

GIRLFRIEND: Good news, seems like I haven't heard good news from you in quite some time.

SEVEN: What does that supposed to mean?

GIRLFRIEND: Come on Seven, don't act like you don't know what I'm talking about.

SEVEN: What, since I've been waking up.

GIRLFRIEND: If that's what you call waking up. Quitting your job, basically throwing everything you worked for away. For what? To wake up? Wake up what Seven? What happened?

SEVEN: Do you believe in me?

GIRLFRIEND: (Long pause) Yes I do.

SEVEN: Do you still love me?

GIRLFRIEND: ...yes, look somebody is calling, I have to take this call. I'll talk to you when you get back.

Seven ends the call with a weird feeling in his gut. He wonders if he has been overlooking the fact that his girlfriend may not be going where he is headed. His love for her doesn't stop her from being conformed to the ways of this world. He leans back in his lawn chair that sinks in the sand. He hears the sliding door of the beach house from behind him. It was Destiny walking to the edge of the balcony. She was looking at Seven and smiling. King walks out from the balcony and downstairs to ground level. He walks towards Seven with his grill shinning and his sister by his side.

SEVEN: What happen?

KING: Will you baptize me?

SEVEN: Right now?

KING: Right now, here in the ocean.

SEVEN: Yea man, I don't know the correct way, or if there is even a correct way, but shoot yea!

DESTINY: Skip the standard way, were having church at the beach.

SEVEN: Right on. God knows our heart.

KING: I rather it happen out here in nature, than at a church. I'm ready to give up all this shit man. I'm tired of hustling, robbing, stealing and selling drugs to my people. I can't be free doing all of that. I'm ready to rest, your boy is tired man.

DESTINY: Thank God!

King takes off his shirt and kicks off his $600 dollar pair of shoes. He walks into the water, while other two followed. Once the ocean water reached waist level is when Seven took over from there. All three held hands while Seven prayed. Destiny stood on one side of King, while Seven stood on the other side. After Seven prays, he asks King the question, "do he accept Jesus Christ as his Lord and Savior," and he replies, "Yes I do." King leans back into their arms, where they bring his body under the water. Once they lifted him back up from the water, he didn't open his eyes right away. King tilts his head back and let out a shout into the sky. A shout of years of pain, frustration, guilt, and suffering.

King opens his eyes and looks up into the dark sky. Destiny wipes the tears in her eyes away, while Seven feels the energy of the holy spirit working. King reaches toward the other two and they all came together and embraced. The three have been deprived of a good loving hug by someone who genuinely loves them until now. Neither one let go.

Chapter **9**

THE GAME CHANGER

The fact of there being witnesses of King and Destiny leaving the hotel, the crew decided to hit the road to be on the safe side. They packed their bags and were on the highway around 2am. They spoke of plans before fatigue started to kick in. King would tell the others to get some rest and that he will wake them up before stopping at the next hotel. He drove the rest of the way while Seven and Destiny were sound of asleep. He thought of his plans while in silence the whole way back. Hours before arriving back home, king calls both Squint and Turtle to get ready to go out to eat.

• • •

Once they arrive back in Dallas, King drives straight to the elder uncles he never had and gave a heartfelt hug to both Turtle and Squint when they all came together. It was the first time he had ever hugged them. There was no need to take two cars, King wanted to go as one big family.

The group of five invaded a Mexican restaurant and sat in a big booth. King ordered all kinds of food, from chips and salsa, enchiladas, fajitas, quesadillas, rice, beans, chicken, beef, shrimp, and steak tacos to go along with a big picture of a frozen margarita. The last supper was the scene, while the cool, laid back Mexican music filled the atmosphere. Before they ate, King told everybody he was going to bless the food. This was the first time he ever did such thing. They all held hands while King spoke a naturally spoken prayer that let Seven know he was not new at this. Destiny held in her tears of joy from feeling that her brother's life was already changing. She knew that he didn't half step anything. If he was in, he went all in. Turtle was such in shocked he didn't even close his eyes for the whole prayer. Before King finished up his brief prayer, the table says, Aman.

SQUINT: What did you guys do to this man on this vacation?

KING: I changed my brother. And I brought you two here, to look you in your eyes and tell you that I'm sorry. I'm sorry for selling you dope. I have played a hand in help destroying you, and that has come to an end. I'll no longer be selling drugs to you two anymore.

Instead, I'm going to dedicate myself to help turn your life around, no matter what it will take. And Destiny and Seven are down to help as well.

TURTLE: That is beautiful King, but it is not that easy man. I've tried shaking these devil drug for years.

KING: I understand, that's why we are all going to help you, and be there for you every step of the way. I'll pay for counseling and a rehab center. I'll drive you to all the classes.

SQUINT: I thank you King, but what if I'm not ready to stop.

KING: Look man, I know I may not be going about this the right way, but I don't give a damn. I'm going to make it up to you and God for having my hand in damaging you.

SQUINT: What if we just find the drug with or without you? Don't blame yourself for our actions. You didn't hold a gun up to our head and force us to hit that crack pipe or snort that line.

KING: I know, but screw that. I love y'all man. Everybody at this table is all I got. And I ride for mines.

TURTLE: I feel you young blood. This is really what we want, but it's that drug that is causing us to fight it. It's a monster man.

SQUINT: And you not going to be able to monitor us 24/7 King.

King: I know that. I know you can get the drug from somebody else, but I'll tell you how for real I am about this. I'm going to find out who is selling to you and I'm going to find them, and instill fear in their heart so much, to where they will run from you when coming around. You got two options, either allow me to get you help, or leave this entire city.

SQUINT: Aw shit, I done lost my appetite.

TURTLE: What happened to you changing?

KING: I have, I'm just a different type of believer. My God is not of a timid God and neither will I be. If I'm wrong in any way, God will deal with me accordingly. But as of right now, it is on my heart to fix what I help destroy.. Look, I'm going to help you. And once you get right and clean, I promise you, I'll move you both in your own apartment that is fully furnished. I'll buy you a good reliable car and have you a decent paying job ready for you. To go with some money in your bank account to maintain until you get some checks rolling in.

DESTINY: Come on my brothers, you can't beat that. I love you too, and want to see you turn it around and be prosperous.

SEVEN: I've been knowing you two for a short amount of time, and I already appreciate your company more than most people that I have ever met. I'm down for the cause fellas.

● ● ●

King wasted no time on his mission to rehabilitate Turtle and Squint. King awoke at sun rise and paid a visit to the nearest rehab center. After working out the details, he paid for rooms in the facility center. When the time came, he intends to pay their minor bills during their stay. The first day to enter the rehabilitation center would begin in one week, so King decided to sign up Turtle and Squint to attend a daily addiction class until then. Monday through Friday starting at 7 to 8 o'clock. Seven went back to work at the library and spent most of his free time completing his first book.

King drives Squint and Turtle to their first meeting and drops them off. He sat in his car and listened to an audio book until the hour passed. The first two days went smooth. There was a positive vibe the first two days. Both Squint and Turtle showed interest in trying to turn their life around. The support from King made a difference in their will to do. His inner guilt caused him to wait on them hand and foot. On the third night, Seven joined King to drop off the old timer's. King always parked close to the building so he could see the front entrance. King played some music on a low volume while the two conversed.

SEVEN: I noticed you haven't smoked any blacks & milds ever since we left Cali.

KING: Yea bro, I can't explain it. I haven't had an urge to smoke.

SEVEN: That's what I'm talking about.

KING: Just somebody noticing it encourages me. How is the book coming along?

SEVEN: It's coming along good. I'm close to finishing the packet.

KING: Yes indeed, finish it with patience and get it out there to the people. I never knew being a blessing to people would feel this good.

SEVEN: Oh yea, especially when it's from the heart.

KING: You may not know it, but you have been a blessing to me. If it wasn't for you I wouldn't be in this position.

SEVEN: (Fist dap with King) Indeed. That means a lot. I can say the same thing about you. It's like God put you in my life to help mold me for something greater later.

KING: I know without a doubt, you are here for a specific purpose and you will do great things by bringing light to this world.

SEVEN: You can see that happening?

KING: I've been around a few people in my life time who have an angel like spirit. Your one of them, on top of having a gift. Let me tell you something man and don't forget this. Everything you have experienced may cause you not to see yourself having a big impact. And it may never happen until you start believing in yourself 100 percent.

SEVEN: I hear you.

KING: I am not telling you nothing that you don't already know, it's just reassurance. Stand firm on whatever it is you want, need and desire with full force. Your greatest strength is your weakness. You are pure, kind, and have a big heart. Stand firm, because this world can take your kindness for weakness. This is what I noticed, at the diner we ate at, you went without having your cup of water refilled for half of your meal. Maybe because you knew the waitress was busy and you didn't want to make it any busier for her. Bro, get that waitress attention and get your cup refilled man. That's her job. When we went shopping, you would like the expensive shirt, but you went with the cheaper shirt. Why, because your heart, you are not selfish, nor do you want for much. I understand, but go with that first option. That's what you wanted, then go get it. Claim it. It's yours. That's nothing but a shirt that cost money, you act like you don't deserve whatever you desire. You deserve it man. You are so humble that you put everybody before you, and you're okay with taking the least so the people around you can be good. That's great, you are a true man of God, but now is the time to take what's yours. It's time for you to go first, time for you to have the most for a change.

SEVEN: Right on, I feel you my brother. I needed to hear that.

KING: Yea man, I see everything. Unfortunately, in this backwards world we live in, that nice guy stuff will only get you so far. Keep being you, but you gotta know when to turn it up and turn it off. What would Jesus do? Jesus was bold, but with compassion and love. And once you realize that, your world will change, and watch how it all comes into fruition. Forget what people think about you, if it got your name on it, be willing to act a fool to get what's yours. What is the worst that can happen?

While looking forward, King spots out Squint walking out the front door of the building. He looks at the time on his watch, and sees that class isn't over until another 30 minutes. Squint spots out King looking right at him and took off running. King swings open his car door and took off running after him. Squint turned the corner of the building and was running for dear life. He looked behind him and saw King gaining on him. "Stop running," he yelled out to the scampering Squint who weaved through and around slides, swings, and a merry go round. Soon as King caught up with him, he dove and tackled him to the ground like a defensive end sacking a quarterback.

KING: What the hell are you doing Squint!

SQUINT: (Breathing hard) I can't do this man, I need a fix.

KING: (While catching his breath) Man get yo ass up.

SQUINT: (Heavy breathing) Hold up, let me lie here for second, I'm tired as hell. My legs are burning.

KING: Don't make me drag your ass all the way back to the meeting.

SQUINT: Don't do me like that, I slipped up. I'm trying! The drug is calling me.

Once King heard that, a great deal of understanding kicked in. He realized that it was going to be a process. He sat down next to Squint and caught his breath.

KING: I know man. But you gotta keep fighting. You are in a war right now and I'm not going to let you lose.

SQUINT: (Hanging his head down)

KING: Get your head up! You got this, your good. I'm with you unc. Can I call you my uncle?

SQUINT: (Lifts his head back up) Yes you can.. alright, I'll keep pushing through.

KING: That's what I'm talking about unc!

SQUINT: Damn, you should have ran track, shit!

King stands to his feet and holds out his hand to help Squint to his feet. They both walk back and Squint returns to class with grass still in his hair and wrinkled clothes. Turtle sees him walk back in and calls him out in front of the class, "damn, who whooped your ass man," while laughing at his friend.

Friday was rocky for the King. He couldn't get ahold of Squint by phone or at his resting place. He continued his search after dropping Turtle off at class. He cruised the streets where there was a high activity of drugs being sold. His straight face was covered by sadness from seeing far too many people walk the streets like zombies. A handful of spiritless bodies roaming the streets in search to get their next fix. A few hustlers and their boy's hung outside on the block, while the money came rolling in. King could spot out the flaws in how they moved as hustler's. He saw them as being to out in the open. There was nothing secretive about how they ran their operation. It was a no brainer for the cops to have reason to believe they are selling drugs.

After King picked up Turtle from class, the search continued. Turtle gave directions to any place Squint could possibly be. There was a cheap motel in the hood where to many tricks and addicts hung out. They asked familiar faces if they have seen Squint. He was pointed in the right direction to the exact room. There was no answer from the people inside the motel room after knocking twice. The door was opened right after King let it be known that he was going to shoot the door knob to get in. He witnessed Squint sitting in a chair high as a kite. He was zoned out until he saw King standing at the door. "Let's go Squint," King spoke. He didn't even try to put up a verbal defense. He just slowly got up and walked to the door while a few others in the room were high out of their mind.

SQUINT: King, I'm sorry man, I am no good.

KING: You don't have to apologize to me unc, I understand it's a fight. But you are going to take me to the person who sold you the dope.

SQUINT: Come on King, you know I can't rat nobody out.

I Am Your Brother

KING: Get out of that street code shit! These streets don't love you. Now, how do you want to handle this? At ease, or with force?

SQUINT: Okay man. Just aggressive with it, geez la weez. It's over there on MLK and Bronze.

TURTLE: You have to be careful over there, them hard head youngsters like to roll in packs.

KING: That's all I needed to know.

King drove straight to the location with no hesitation. He could feel both Turtle and Squint's energy of fear rising. He didn't speak the rest of the way. He turned his music up loud while bobbing his head to some chopped and screwed Z-RO. Soon as they drove passed Bronze Street, Squint pointed out Tre D who sold him the dope. All King needed to hear was the name. He noticed there was about six of his boys and two young ladies with him. They were drinking and smoking while standing by the front porch. King drives up a couple more blocks and makes a u-turn before parking the car. He gets out of the car and tells Turtle to get into the drivers seat.

KING: Okay here is the play, I want you to drive and wait for me to tell you where to park. Keep the car running. Once I let it be known, to never sell to you two again, we don't know how they will react. So I need yall to play it cool and be on high alert.

The area was dark. Kings demeanor didn't change one bit like he had ice in his veins. Turtle drives down

Martin Luther King Street and makes the turn on Bronze Street. He drives closer to the house where the group hung out. King tells Squint to park right in the middle of the street and put the car in park. The unfamiliar car that stops in the middle of the street causes the men and two women to stand to their feet. One puts his hand on his gun, while a couple others squint their eyes to see who was driving the car. King steps out of the car.

KING: I come in peace, tame that dog. I'm looking for Tre D.

TRE D: Yea who wants to know?

KING: I want to know.

He walks away from the car and moves closer to the group of men with frowning faces. King turns back and tells Squint and Turtle to get out of the car. Once they are out of the car, Tre D recognizes both of them. King tells them both to get back into the car.

KING: With all due respect, but those two men right there, that's my family, and I'm asking you to never sell dope to them again.

TRE D: (Looks at his boys before responding back) What are you the dope police trying to block me from making my paper?

KING: Not at all, just trying to see my people live. That's all I'm asking, not to sell to these two. Can you do that for me?

Tre D knows his boys and the two ladies are closely watching him to see his reaction. They weren't used to anybody pulling up on them like this.

TRE D: Yo blood, who you think you are pulling up on my block trying to call shots like you the boss. Step off for we run you off.

Squint almost wet his pants from being scared. Turtle shakes his head and prepares to perform the request of King. King remains silent while just staring Tre D at a distance. He turns around and starts walking back towards his car. One of the girls started laughing at King, while one of the youngsters spoke fly words as King was walking away. King walked up to the driver's door and told Turtle to turn the Z Ro song all the way up. He bobbed his head up and down from feeling the rap song. In his usual cool, calm, and collective demeanor, he took off his watch and handed it to Turtle. He takes off his collared polo shirt and neatly folded it and handed it to Turtle once more. He bent over and retied both of his shoes laces to fit tight on his feet. As he stood up, in his mind he asks God to be with him. His tall slim muscular frame turned around and walks back towards Tre D and his boys.

KING: Check me out, you can either respect my wishes, or step out in this street and get your ass beat. And after I knock yo ass out, any of your homies can line it up and get their ass beat one by one. And if you boys jump me, you better kill me. Cause if not, I'll be back and air this block out, and have first 48 in this bitch. So what's the damn deal, I'm prepared to die tonight.

Soon as King could see just a bit of fear in Tre D's eyes, he knew he had them. Their tough guy radar decreased within seconds. The woman stopped laughing and the fly talk came to an end. Now, it was just a matter of getting his point across.

KING: If don't nobody want no problems, then I'll be on my way. I didn't come here to cause drama. Just don't sell dope to my family. You not real G's if you don't respect what I'm saying. I pray for you youngsters out here man. But don't have me come back over here or it will be a different script written.

Tre D and his boys were silent. The two ladies there with them just got of glimpse of the real thing. Turtle moves over to the passenger seat and King gets in. After driving off and turning a few corners, King noticed Turtle with tears in his eyes and Squint with his head buried in his praying hands. King turns down his music.

KING: What's up?

SQUINT: You really love us man. It's hurting me to disappoint you.

TURTLE: Nobody ever went to bat for me like that.

It hit King like never before. All three men lacked love throughout their life. King pulled the car over in the nearest parking lot and parks. He tells them to all hold hands so he could pray. He prayed for the spirit of God to take the urge of their addiction to be removed. He asked for forgiveness and for God to lead them in the right direction. The energy inside the car gave Turtle and Squint chills through their body. After the prayer, King lets it be known that he was there for the long haul, and that he would ride for them through the good and the bad.

The long night eventually came to an end. Destiny was relaxed out in her room, while King sat in his man cave. He looked at the television while not paying any attention to it. He dozed off before a bad dream awoke him. He was breathing hard and began to sweat. He walks by Destiny's room and sees that she was sleep. He walks next to her bed, stretches out his hand and silently prays for her. He stares for moment before leaving her room. He calls Seven to check on him. He asks him come over Sunday night so he could give him something. Before ending the brief conversation, he tells Seven that he loved him like a brother. He then takes out a pen and writes a note on a small piece of paper.

King hardly spoke the next couple of days. Saturday he stayed in his man cave and watched old YouTube fights of Floyd Mayweather and a couple of his favorite movies. He cooked his favorite two dishes, one for Saturday and the other for Sunday dinner. He received a text from Turtles phone, asking if he could go pick him up from being stranded. King gave it a thought before responding back. He didn't ask any questions, just text back where he needed to be picked up at. King tells Destiny that he would be right back and that Seven was on his way. He usually would take his everyday get around car, but he oddly chose to take the Cadillac. King drives to the location that happened to be not far from his home. He enjoyed every moment of the ride. He smiles at the kids he passed by and even waved the peace sign at a walking stranger. He appreciated the stars in the dark sky, while simply being thankful for the smallest of things. From the air that he breathed, to having all his five senses in tact.

Once he arrived at the location, he parked the car on the side of the street and texted Turtle that he arrived. He rolled his window down and waited for a response. About one minute later he gets a text back from Turtle that reads, "LEAVE NOW, IT'S A SETUP." King rereads the text and starts the engine. Out of nowhere, he sees Tre D from behind the car walk up to the driver's window, "remember me," and sticks out a 45 caliber gun at King and pulls the trigger three times before running off. Screams from people who heard the gun shots. King clutches his chest and leans over to the side and isn't moving for a moment. His life flashed before his eyes. He used all his strength to raise himself back up. He drove away while his vision blurred in and out. He sped back to his house, while swerving the car from a lack of concentration. All you could hear was a car out of control by side swiping a few cars that were parked on the side of the street. Hitting the cars shifted his body around as if he was on a rocky roller coaster ride.

Seven is dropped off at Kings house by his uber driver. When walking to the front door he could hear all the loud crashing noise from down the street. To his surprise, it was the black Cadillac recklessly slide swiping cars that were parked on the sideup the street. King runs over the curb before pulling into the drive way. He parks and staggered out with his shirt soaked in blood. He stumbled to the front porch and fell into Sevens arms before falling to the ground. Seven was in a state of shock, while King was gasping for air. King used the rest of his will and energy to reach in his pocket and pull out the small piece of paper and handed it to Seven. "Do it now," King manages to speak with his eyes starting to roll in the back of his head. "Hold on the blood in his mouth. King smiles at Seven, "You saved me."

Police sirens were approaching from afar. Destiny approaches the door and sees her brother laid out on the ground covered in blood. Her knees buckle as she almost faints. She slowly falls to her knees next to her dying brother. King put the palm of his hand on Destiny's face and smiled. His hand dropped from her face. She could feel King take his last breath. She cries out so loud the whole block could hear her pain.

Seven scoots back and gives Destiny the time with her brother. Although his mind was gone, he had to think fast before the police showed up. His mind raced 100 miles per hour while holding the piece of paper in his hand. He remembered King telling him, "do it now." He unfolds the small piece of paper and the words read.

"If you are reading this, I'm no longer here in the physical and I left something for you inside my safe.

Look out for Destiny for me. Peace and love brother. 11-11-33"

Tears streamed down his face. He gets up and runs towards Kings man cave. He could hear the sirens getting closer and closer. He knew that he must move fast and gather himself before it was too late. He searched around the room frantically for the safe. The sirens were moving in closer. He scrambles into the closet where he can see the secret place where King kept the safe. He enters the code digits on the piece of paper and the door opens. A black backpack was the only thing inside. He grabs the bag and runs back outside to a crying Destiny who laid hugging Kings lifeless body. Seven puts the backpack on and begins to pick up King from the ground. "We have to leave fast Destiny. I'm so sorry. We have to leave now. Help me put him in the car." Destiny knew if the cops came and start investigating, then everything they worked for could be put in jeopardy. They both pick King up and put him inside the back seat. Seven stayed in the back with King, while Destiny got into the driver's seat and drove off right in time before the cops showed up.

DESTINY: God don't take my brother. Take me instead God. (Speeds to the nearest hospital)

SEVEN: I'm so sorry Destiny, but you have to focus for me okay. Stay with me. You have to drop me off at the emergency room, and take the car and get of the here fast. Destiny straightened up, while tears streamed down her face. Seven decides to open the backpack and look inside. Soon as he unzipped the bag and smells money. There was stacks upon stacks of money inside with a note on top. He takes out the note and reads..

"This is all the money I made from robbing people. I believe it was all meant to give to you. You will know what to do with it. It's your time now."

Seven zips the bag up and looks at the face of King. He knew how smart King was, but it just hit him of how brilliant and calculative he truly was. Just when he found a true friend who understood him, he passes away. He wasn't ready for him to go. He wanted more and needed more of the big brother he never had. Sadness got a hold of his heart. He wipes the blood of King with his hand and just stares at it. He closes his fist tight and watches the blood squeeze out and run down his arm.

The beat-up Cadillac drives into the entrance of the emergency room. Destiny gets out and hugs her brother for the last time. Seven lifts King on his shoulder and walks inside the building. "I need a doctor now!" Two nurses rush to bring the rolling stretcher. He meets them half way and lies the King down on his back. Seven keeps his head low to avoid eye contact with the nurses. He put his forehead on Kings forehead, "rest in power my brother, may your spirit be my guardian angel." He grips the straps of the backpack, turns away and walks toward the exit.

Chapter 10

THE MASTER PLAN

CHAPTER 1 FLASHBACK TAKES PLACE NOW

Seven sits at the back of the bus and stares out the window. The scattered blood on his clothing brought unwanted attention. There was no way to disappear, so he sat there and faced the music. All within hours, the death of King, catching his girlfriend with another man and a backpack filled with hundreds of thousands of dollars. Not even the money could boost his drained spirit. The blood on his clothing has caused a cautious energy inside the bus. The last thing he wanted was for anyone to be overly concerned, or fearful enough to call the cops. His urge to be safe than sorry caused him to get off at the next stop. He takes off the red stained shirt and throws it into a trash can along the way. There was a little blood on his white undershirt, but not noticeable enough to bring attention.

The heavy hearted backpacker traveled nine miles before arriving home. He walks inside and goes straight to the shower. He leans his forehead against the wall, while watching the blood of King rinse into the drain. Asking himself, "what is really going on?" He lets the phone charge up while thinking of what to say to Destiny. She didn't answer his call, nor did she respond back to his text messages. He stressed himself to sleep. Days would pass with no sign of her. He remained inside with no desire to leave. Once to the grocery store and two late night visits to the library all within a month. The last words of King played in his mind throughout the day. What did he mean by, "you will know what to do with it," Seven thought to himself? He read throughout his journals and analyzed for any clues. He thinks about the talks during the road trip. Left to wonder in an apartment that became his cell. He started exercising like King did when being locked inside the hole. The more he meditated, prayed and was still, the more he felt in-tuned to his talents, gifts, and desires. He studied so much to where he brought a comforter, blanket and pillow to the library.

In the mist of evolving, he spent much time staring out his apartment window. The forgotten world, so it seemed. But there was something special about the people who lived in the place they call, the hood. He experienced the feel it gives when having the least or facing the pressures of going without. From the thoughts that arrive, to the anger that is available to receive. From what it can do psychologically of consistently seeing the cops red and blue flashing lights in your neighborhood, to the sorrow of seeing another one who looks like you being handcuffed and taken off in the back of a police car. From having the least, but yet the most talent. Besides the people outside his window being the most down to earth that he has encountered, the idea of the people being given an equal chance as the more fortunate greatly intrigued him. Especially, with an unbreakable spirit, despite all that one is up against.

More time has passed and still no word from Destiny June. He began to miss her dearly. There wasn't an hour that passed by without thinking of her. To make matters worse, his only contact number was no longer a valid number. He just knew in his mind that she moved far away and changed her number. Why would she stay when being hunted he assumed. He didn't understand why every person that he had ever wanted more of was taken away from him.

After forty days of being out of sight and out of mind, he felt like he received a vision that moved his spirit. He asked no more questions, nor did he think twice about it. He simply moved. The first move was to call rehab centers to see about Turtle and Squint possibly being there. Once he was informed that Squint was at a particular location, he called his Uber driver Diego to drop him off for a visit. He waited in a visiting area outside the rehab facility. Once Squint walked around the corner they both smiled before hugging each other. It was the first time Seven smiled in quite sometime. Squint looked healthier than before. A drastic change was evident by the energy of his presence.

SEVEN: Man who is this guy!

SQUINT: Well, if it isn't the angelic Seven.

SEVEN: My goodness it is good to see you. You look great man.

SQUINT: Thank you, I feel good. Haven't felt like this in years.

SEVEN: You've just brought me a great joy that greatly needed. Hey, how about we take a walk and talk.

(The two talk while the birds chirped and squirrels dashed the yard)

SEVEN: It's good seeing you. I haven't seen anybody since King passed. Not even from Destiny. I took it pretty hard but I'm feeling better each day.

SQUINT: Yea, it hit home for me too. He saved me. I wanted to go smoke my life away after he passed, but his passing is the only reason why I'm here trying to turn my life around. You know once an addict, always an addict they say, but I have it in my mind that I don't ever want to go back to drugs. After King prayed with me and Turtle, I had less of an urge to hit that pipe, but once he passed it just really made me want to totally stop. I know that is what he wanted and this is my dedication for him.

SEVEN: That's beautiful. I'm so proud of you. I really am. What about Turtle, I couldn't locate him.

SQUINT: Not so good I believe. Do you know how everything went down?

SEVEN: No, I just know he was shot.

Squint would go on and tell how the whole setup went down. From King confronting Tre D about not selling dope to Turtle or Squint any more, to how the pride of Tre D came into play after being called out and backing down. From Tre D kidnapping Turtle, to beating him half to death for not telling him where he could find King. How Turtle mentioned that he couldn't take the beating no more, and how he finally gave in after Tre D held the gun to his head. That is when they set up King by texting him with Turtles phone, texting that he needed a ride home. King drove over to pick up Turtle and that is when Tre D approached his car and shot him. Once Tre D left to attack King, is when Turtle texted King to get out of there, but it was too late.

Once Turtle knew King was dead, he just couldn't take it and mentally checked out. He tried to stay at rehab, but he was just too torn up from having a hand in King's death. After telling Squint goodbye, that was the last anyone heard or seen from Turtle. Seven plays everything out in his mind and keeps strong from crying. He knew Turtle was in a tough situation and didn't fault him for his actions. Just a bad situation all together, but at least he would not have to wonder the cause of death anymore. They both talked for another hour before Seven left. Squint mentioned that he could leave whenever he wanted to go visit friends so keep in contact. Until then, he was going to remain at the rehab center until he totally felt 100 percent confident in his recovery.

Seeing the change in Squint inspired Seven to put the finishing touches on his first book project and get it out there to the people. Soon as he made it home he worked on the book nonstop, while starring out his apartment window in between breaks. He hardly slept and just snacked around here and there. He completed the writing process of the book within the next two days. He used some money from the black backpack to buy all the materials he needed to turn his words into a book form. He bought the paper, printer, ink cartridges and whatever else he needed to make it presentable for the reader.

The book consists of health tips on a proper diet. It breaks down what foods were essential for us and the ones we needed to stay away from. It goes into the pH levels of the body. How we become sick once it enters an acidic state vs, how to keep your body in a alkaline state. It breaks down how diseases form in the body. It breaks down the causes of many symptoms, and how to go about getting rid of the symptoms. It breaks down steps on how to heal yourself through a proper diet, fasting, meditation, faith, and prayer. It touches up on some of the causes of GMO's (genetically modified organism), processed foods and the over consumption meat. How diseases maintains by feeding off the toxins and decay in the body, and how the benefits of stop feeding the disease, will eventually starve itself out. He goes in depth about the wonders of alkaline water, lemons, fruits, vegetables, sea moss, and many other live foods that come from the earth. He backs his facts up by scripture and health statistics. He purposely decides not to get the book copy written or published. He wanted this project to have nothing to do with any type of government, overseer, or big corporate company that is connected to the the problem. He was now realizing that the time has come.

He spent 18 out the 24 hours of the day manually putting the book together. He used 100's, 50's and 20 dollar bills as a book mark inside each book. He puts on a black hoodie and backpack full of books inside. He takes a deep breath before stepping outside and makes the first move of actioin. You could put Seven in a class of master's when it came to reading and feeling the energy of people. He walked around the neighborhood looking for people to bless. Carefully selected one by one he gave out a book. The ones who he felt in the most need, are the ones he gave a book with the 100 dollar book markers inside. He didn't take credit when being thanked, "glory be to God," was his respond back. He would tell certain people to not mention it to anyone as if he was a ghost. Although he was telling the people to keep it on the low, he knew the word would slowly but surely spread.

Seven found himself wanting to get out and catch a late night movie. He was accustomed to going to the movie theater alone. He liked to catch the latest movie time when the theater had less people there. The parking lot was almost empty when being dropped off by his Uber driver. He pays for his movie ticket, buys a small popcorn, and non- carbonated drink before making his way in theater room number seven. As he made his way up the ramp and turned the corner, he noticed a woman sitting in his favorite seating area in the middle of the theater. He found it to be odd, but continued to walk towards the back seating. The previews came on soon as he found his seat. The light from the preview shedded more light on the women who sat alone.

A strong feeling of curiosity came to him as he looked at the woman closer. She then turned and looked at Seven where they both starred at one other at a distance. The woman happened to be Destiny June. The look of surprise in both of their eyes. Seven got up from his seat and walked to the edge of the row where she was sitting. He stood there for a moment, just to make sure his eyes were not deceiving him. And it was so. You couldn't tell by her facial expression but she became more alive when seeing him. Seven walked about three seats away from her and stopped before speaking. Destiny stands to her feet as they both starred into each other's eyes. The back view of the theater was the standing silhouette of Seven and Destiny facing each other in the middle of big movie screen.

SEVEN: Hello there, my name is Seven. I don't believe we met before.

DESTINY: ... Hello, my name is Destiny.

SEVEN: I like that name. Hey this might sound weird, but do you mind if I join you for this movie?

DESTINY: (Looks around the empty theater and smiles) Sure, I would like that. But only if you don't like to talk the whole movie.

Seven grins while holding out his hand, "nice to meet you Destiny." She shakes his hand back, "nice to meet you as well." There was a great silent satisfaction of seeing one another and playing the role of a strangers. It felt right, so they rolled with it. They spoke as cool movie watchers until the previews ended. No matter the act, the energy was felt. They didn't speak the whole movie, only glanced at each other a couple times. The brown eyed, natural hair wearing, melinated woman was gorgeous in the most unwanted need for attention type of way.

They walked out of the theater together sharing thoughts on the movie. She couldn't help but to notice how nice they looked together when seeing their reflection in the class door exit. Once outside the building, they stopped and turned to face each other before going their own separate ways. A light drizzle of rain began to fall from the sky. He didn't hesitate by asking if he could continue hanging out with her. Just the words she wanted to hear. To his surprise, she opens Sevens door and let him in. That happened to be a first for the natural charmer who shows his appreciation.

• • •

Seven didn't have plans of bringing up the loss of King until she was ready to. She was now alone in this world with options of doing whatever she wanted. When driving closer to her home she notices an unusual car parked near her house on the opposite side of the street. Seven was preparing himself to see the very spot where he last saw King take his last breath. But Destiny kept driving once she noticed the steak out man being the big muscular guy from the north side . She specifically remembers him from the night that everything changed. She was used to feeling numb the last month of her life to where seeing the man didn't startle her. She mentally accepted it right away and knew it was time to think of a plan. She kept driving while looking straight ahead hoping the north side guy didn't see her. She turned onto the nearest street to get out of sight.

SEVEN: Are you okay?

DESTINY: One of the north side boys were back there steaking out.

SEVEN: I figured that's why you kept driving. We can go to my place if you like, until you decide your next move.

DESTINY: My goodness, I thought that was the end of those guys. Well, it comes with territory. Once I get passed these guys, I'll be free of all of this past life of mine. I'm done with that life style.

SEVEN: We.. when we get passed it. I'm here, you don't have to do it alone.

Seven was a breath of fresh air to her. He put his hand over her hand and said that everything was going to be okay. The light drizzle turned to rain, and rain back to a light sprinkle when traveling to their destination.

DESTINY: I don't think it's appropriate for me to be over at this time of night, I don't think your girlfriend would approve.

SEVEN: You speak of the woman I caught with another man. She no longer matters.

DESTINY: Okay, I'm just ready to lay down.

Lightening illuminates the sky when Seven gets out of the car and takes over the driving duties. Once they made it on his side of town, things got more interesting. Seven whitnesses a police car parked near the section of his apartment building. He continues to drive closer to the entrance way of his building. While strolling closer, he sees the officer wearing an eye patch standing in the breeze way. Low and behold it was the policeman he made eye contact with when leaving the emergency room. To avoid driving passed the cop, he quickly turns into the first open parking spot. He stays calm to not make it look obvious that he was dodging the cop. He puts the car in reverse and backs out of the parking spot while watching to see if the officer noticed them. Destiny can see that the officer was eye balling her car all the way to exiting the parking lot.

DESTINY: Is he looking for you?

SEVEN: Possibly. We walked passed each other after leaving the hospital. But then again, things happen over here all the time, could be just a coincidence.

DESTINY: I can't take this, it's too much right now.

SEVEN: Don't worry, I'm not going to let anything happen to you.

DESTINY: They are looking for the both of us.

Seven could tell he was dealing with a different Destiny now that King was out of her life. She finally showed signs of not being indestructible.

SEVEN: Before you know it, this is all going to be over soon. This is just a part in your movie.

The rain gradually comes pouring down harder. It was late and Seven could feel that Destiny was very tired. She didn't ask any questions by following his lead. He took her to a place where he knew they would be safe. He drives to the library that is not too far from his apartment. The rain is pouring down, mixed with the occasional sounds of thunder and lightning. He parks in the back of the building, takes her hand and they run to the back door of the building. Soon as they enter and close the door behind them, the sound of loud rain has now become the instrumental of stormy night. The smell of books, fresh plants, and wooden shelves filled the air as Seven walks her to his spot. She stays close by his side from barely being able to see in the dark room. He lit a candle and tells her to wait there as he stepped away for a moment. He returns with a T-shirt, a pillow and a thick comforter that doesn't make laying on the ground so bad. He made sure he had what he needed from the many nights he would sleep in the library.

Just as Seven seen another side of Destiny, she too was seeing another side of him. He took charge with consideration. He was direct and sure of himself with his actions. He walks her near the row of tall book shelves. Seven stands on one side of the book shelf so they wouldn't see each other change clothes, while Destiny stood on the other side. Seven removes a section of books so he could see Destiny's face from the other side. Rain drops tapped on the roof on the building while the candle lit dims the scene.

SEVEN: There you are.

DESTINY: Hey big head.

SEVEN: Hey beautiful.

DESTINY: (Blushes) What I tell you about beautiful being overrated?

SEVEN: That was before I got to know you. And beauty is what I see.

DESTINY: Do you want to know more about me?

SEVEN: Since the first time I laid eyes on you I've wanted to.

DESTINY: ... I've been so alone.

SEVEN: Me too.

DESTINY: I don't know what to do from here.

SEVEN: Let go and trust me.

DESTINY: What does that mean Seven?

SEVEN: You know that feeling you have right now towards me?

DESTINY: Yes.

SEVEN: Just go with it.

They stare into each other's eyes from the opposite sides of the book shelve that separates them. Seven leaves from where he stood standing and Destiny follows his lead. Once they meet at the end of the book shelve, they fall into each other's arms and passionately kiss. He lifts her up and she wraps her legs around his waist. He walks her to the blanket and gently lays her down. They kissed each others lips, while holding each other close. Destiny was on one accord with the frequency of being in the moment, but the considerate soul of Seven remembered her saying how she wanted her first time to be, and so he respected her wishes by keeping that dream alive and not taking it further. His spirit was leading him to be patient with her, and by doing so will be key as they grow together. Besides, the moment felt priceless, being the best he has felt in a long time. He thought that he would never be able to see Destiny again. The two held each other until she fell asleep in his arms. The sound of rain, the ambience of candle light, and the two laying together being surrounded by a world of books was the movie scene. The candle goes out while Seven thinks of his master plan.

Chapter

11

THE DEGREELESS HEART
SURGEON

Seven works a rubik's cube while sitting at his desk. His chair faces the bed with the backpack full of money. He thought of the brilliance and bravery of King. From owning his house, cars, and still have so much money left over. The discipline it would take to go all in and execute his plan. The freedom to fly to different states and be with beautiful women whenever he chose. Being your own boss and going by your own rules. His heavy heart added more fuel to his fire. Something you could feel when looking into his eyes. He sat like a sniper hours before the attempted kill, just as King would. Without noticing, Seven was moving similar to King, but yet still being himself. Despite the financial increase, he chose not to buy a car right away. He calls an Uber driver to assist him to buying a ladder and basketball net. After buying the net and ladder, he returned home and prepared to execute the mission. Readiness was in his eyes, like a boxer making his way down the entrance to the ring. He stands by the front door, "God, may your will be done," and walks out.

The sound of screeching sneakers on a black top and a ball bouncing becomes louder as Seven approaches the court in his apartments. With a ladder in one hand, and a net in the other, he stands on the sideline and watches the pickup game. The game being played by all teenagers stopped play and begin to watch Seven. "You brothers mind if I put up this net?" "No we don't mind, go ahead," the smallest players on the court responds back. Seven places the ladder and steps on to reach the netless rim. The teens just stare at him. "Mr, do you work in these apartments?" "No, I just thought maybe you guys would like to play with a net on the rim." The teens look a little confused. "I'm taking the first shot when the net is up," one of the youngsters said while shooting the ball in the air to himself. Seven climbs back down and looked at the group of teens.

YOUNGSTERS: Good looking out man.

SEVEN: You are welcome. Who was winning the game?

YOUNGSTERS: Were up by two.

SEVEN: Alright will check this out. I have a one hundred dollar bill for each player on the winning team, and fifty dollars for each player on the losing team. And I'm going to sit back and watch you ballers get down from the side.

YOUNGSTERS: Whaaat, are you serious right now! Don't be playing with us man.

SEVEN: (Took out some cash from his pocket) Let's play some ball. 0 to 0, let's go.

The youngsters got excited and started while a few shouted, "heyyy," and "let's go!" A few began to tighten up the laces in their shoes.

SEVEN: But wait a minute now, I want to see some balling. I'm not trying to see a bunch of arguing and crying over calls. If so, let me know now.

YOUNGSTERS: Naw were good sir, won't be none of that. Hey, you heard the man, so don't come with all of that crying. Yall mess my money up and were gonna have problems!

Seven carried the ladder off the court and had a seat on the bench. The competitive drive stepped up once money was on the line. He wondered if these kid's knew what it felt like to get an allowance of any kind. If they have received money for making good grades. If not, he wondered if that ever affected their performance in school. He wondered while watching white on rice defense on every possession. A talented bunch indeed, the heart and skill was evident. The game was tight all the way until the end before the game winning bucket sealed the deal. The winning team cheered amongst themselves while the losing team showed their disappointment.

SEVEN: Get your head up young men. That was a good hard fought game. You guys come here and let me ask you something.

They gathered in front of Seven and gave him their undivided attention. Seven pulls out the money in his pocket and hands out one hundred dollar bills to both the winner and losing team. The smiles on their faces touched him so much that chills ran through his body. The youngster's interest in Seven deepened when receiving their reward. The respect caused them to pay more attention to what he was about to say.

SEVEN: Think of how you were playing the game before there was no money involved, and now think of how you started playing the game once you found out the winner would win money. That feel you had, once you realized you could gain something by going hard to get the victory. If you take that same drive you had once the money was involved and apply it to making good grades in school, you would all make straight A's. If you just apply some of the efforts and put it towards being a good brother, son, student, and friend your journey through life will be so much easier. By doing so, you will avoid getting grounded, suspended, whooped, put in jail, and having setbacks that won't be fun. I know life is about learning and we will make some mistakes, but if you know and have the knowledge and wisdom beforehand, you can prevent a lot of drama in life. You don't have to get put in prison to learn your lesson, you can gain it right now. Read and ask questions so you can gain wisdom.

Look at your friend next to you, see that friend as your brother. Be loyal and trust worthy. Treat him how you would want to be treated. I am assuming you all go to the same school. This thought came over me when watching you guys play. What if this group right here played on the same team all through grade school and end up winning the state championship? Because your teamwork, chemistry and bother hood. That is great, but you know what will make it even greater? When people read the articles about how exceptional of young men you are. How they didn't become a product of their environment. How they made A's and B's all through high school. There not just great athletes, but they are great student athletes. Man, you will have all kinds of colleges coming to watch you play. They are looking for student athlete's to give full scholarships to. It don't even have to be for basketball, you can apply it to anything you want to be. You feel me?

YOUNGSTERS: (silence and taking everything in) Yea I feel that sir. That's real respect right there.

SEVEN: Hey, before I get out of here, let me ask you guys a question. How many of you young brothers have a single parent mom at home?

Six out of the eight signaled that they did indeed. That is when Seven opened up his backpack and pulled out eight books.

SEVEN: Do you think your parents could use some extra help with bills or food?

YOUNGSTERS: Seem like we could use some extra help all the time sir. It's a constant struggle out here, we just maintain and deal with the hand we have been dealt with.

SEVEN: Can I trust you brothers to give this book to your mothers?

YOUNGSTERS: Yes you can sir, she would be happy if I gave her some money.

Seven took two hundred dollars and put it inside each book and handed it out to every youngster that stood in front of him. The teens were lost for words before one broke the silence. "Yo who are you sir?"

SEVEN: I am your brother... now, I want you all to pass the integrity test and make sure your mother's get that 200 inside that book.

YOUNGSTERS: Yea yea we got you. And we thank you for everything my brother.

Seven: I'll see yall around, much peace and love family.

Seven mentally says a prayer for each teen when shaking their hand. He could see the appreciation in their brown eyes. The group of teens stood there and watched Seven walk away. The teens wore a look of being stunned, confused, and amazed. For Seven, just knowing the memory will be remembered for the rest of their days was a priceless feeling for him. He wanted to make sure the words he spoke were key.

Seven walks the neighborhood with his senses on sniper mode. His discernment was on high voltage, frequency fully charged, and laser beam radar reader in place. "Lead me God, lead me," he spoke in his mind, while traveling with no specific destination in mind. It wasn't long before he spotted out the neighborhood prostitute sashaying around the street corner. He did not see her as that name, he saw a sister who has become a victim. Seven was good at leaving the judging up to God. Who knows the root problem that led the woman to be a prostitute. He believed that he would have to walk in her shoes in order to do so. The only thing that mattered was the present time.

Prostitute named LEXUS: Hey daddy, you looking for a good time?

SEVEN: No thank you Queen. How are you doing?

LEXUS: Oh so nice of you, he called me Queen. I'm doing good babe.

SEVEN: Are you really good though? With all due respect, I find that hard to believe.

LEXUS: And why so?

SEVEN: It's Just something I feel. And unfortunately, I don't think you are happy about being out here on this corner. But what if I told you a change could happen at this very moment.

LEXUS: Oh is that right? Well, I'm all ears.

SEVEN: I don't want to have a good time, but I do want to pay you for your time. Not only will I pay for your time, I'll pay you to be honest to me.

LEXUS: That sounds like a deal. How much are we talking because my time ain't free.

SEVEN: Whatever you make in a day, I'll double if you hear me out over lunch. I know this diner that's pretty good. I'll put half in your hand now, and give you the rest after we eat.

LEXUS: Let me see the money. I need to make sure your not just slick talking me.

SEVEN: I don't want to flash money out in the open, follow me.

After they walk out of sight Seven hands her the money. Satisfaction mixed with a bit of confusion, "let's go eat, I'm all ears babe," she responds back. Seven calls an Uber driver for the ride. They arrive at the same diner that King took him to. Once they were dropped off, Seven puts a fifty dollar bill inside a book and tells the Uber driver to read page eleven. He noticed a reddish rash on the forearm of the driver.

Seven knew he was going to need consistent rides, so he wanted to build a good rapport with just one driver. Especially, after finding out the main area that the driver covered was in the vicinity of his apartment. He wanted it to where, at anytime the driver sees Seven's number pop up, that it was understood that a big tipper was calling. He didn't want several Uber drivers wondering about his business. He didn't want the suspicion, or the idea of him continuously needing rides to go buy things floating around. Seven learned that when a drug addict doesn't have enough for the next hit, things can become savage. And loose lips can lead the very one in need to Seven. With wanted less chatter in the streets as possible, his plan was to get in good with just one driver.

Workers inside the diner greet Seven as he and Lexus walk inside. The words of King played in his mind, "once they know you are a good tipper, your power in the establishment rises." From wearing a hospital gown, to now walking in with a dolled up prostitute. The young handsome gentleman pulled the chair out for Lexus to sit down. The same waitress from last visit walked over to serve their table. Seven was unbothered by the looks received from being accompied by a prostitute. The attire of Lexus didn't allow her to escape the reality. She felt more comfortable seeing that Seven wasn't ashamed of being seen with her.

SEVEN: Lexus, it's time to get off that corner. That chapter of your life is over. I know it's easier said than done, but I'm going to help you get started.

LEXUS: And how are you going to do that huh?

SEVEN: Do you want to continue on doing this. Does this make you happy?

LEXUS: ...no it doesn't make me happy.. I feel worthless inside.

SEVEN: What's the price you would take to leave the streets?

LEXUS: Why do you want to help me? What's in it for you?

SEVEN: No strings attached. I just want to help. Now, answer my question. What is the price to never go back to selling your body? Take some time off and get yourself together. You could go visit your favorite people. Do you have any kids?

LEXUS: (Begins to tear up while maintaining a straight face) Yes, they probably hate me. I let them down.. Once I started using drugs awhile back, that is when everything fell apart.

SEVEN: So that's the plan. I give you the money, you get yourself together, and go start a relationship with your kid's. Go get them back. And if they don't accept you at first, you swallow your pride and remain consistent at attempting. Time heals all wounds and it's never too late. And you never know the plans of God.

LEXUS: (Wipes her tears with a napkin) I would love that, but I'm just.. I'm stuck.

SEVEN: Where does your kids live?

LEXUS: In a totally different city than me.

(It wasn't long before the waitress comes and places their food on the table)

SEVEN: That's even better. You need a different change of scenery. You take this money I'm going to give you, and take a bus there and find a hotel to stay in. Get you some rest and find yourself. It's time to hit the reset button and start over. Before you know it, your life will have changed.

LEXUS: Why would you do that for a stranger?

SEVEN: Would eight thousand dollars be enough? I give you eight grand right now. To get on the bus and get out of here. You'll be closer to your kids.

LEXUS: (Fans her eyes to keep herself from crying) Got me in here crying and shit. Your taking a big risk young man. I could accept this money and continue doing my thing. How would you know, unless you stalk me.

SEVEN: I believe you can do it. I just have a feeling.

LEXUS: (Just stares at Seven across the table) You really mean that don't you?

SEVEN: I most certainly do.

LEXUS: A rare one you are. A pure heart in this world can be a lot to carry. Especially, when being easy on the eyes. Let me guess, you have to be very careful with women because your love is the real thing. And now you come like a thief in the night and sweep me off my feet, just to change my life.

Seven makes eye contact with his waitress at a distance. He signals for her assistence and respectfully requests for his glass to be refilled. He watches the water being poured in his cup when the half dressed woman across from him speaks, "I'm ready to get away from here. I accept your offer. I don't want to live like this anymore." The good news brought a needed joy to the wounded soldier. It seemed like yesterday, he and King sat in the very same diner. His hidden emotion of saddness was covered by his ambition to carry out his mission. The two continue to talk while finishing their meal. Seven would collect all the information he needed to set up the moving arrangements. He wanted it to where all she had to do was get on the bus and go. He leaves a generous tip on the table and the odd couple leaves the diner.

Destiny didn't hide her pain when Seven came around at times. He was used to seeing the flawless women in total control, to now seeing her at her worst. She didn't put up much of a fight in battling her depression. There were days she didn't get out of bed. All the lights in the room would remain off. Some days she didn't bother to bathe or brush her teeth. She didn't posses the will to move far away when knowing it was best for her. She lacked the energy to go through the whole process of finding a new home out of state. She remained in a hotel on the opposite side of the metroplex for the time being. She took all the time needed in adjusting to life after the death of King. She believed the hurt that she felt was karma from the life she once lived. Although the victims had it coming, she was still involved in the life of set ups, manipulation, hustling, conning, and theft. The aftermath of it all caused her to look back over her shoulder when being out into the world. Her mind was ready to move far away, but her body didn't have the gas to run.

Seven was the only thing that could make Destiny feel better. She was surprised of how great it felt to be held by someone who genuinely cared for her. The more time spent toghether, the more their desire to become one increased. Her virgin hormones tested her patience, while the considerate Seven did not attempt to push the envelope. The self control that he possessed enhanced her desire for him. She was yet to meet a heart like his. For the first time of her adult life, she wondered if she was good enough for a man. The goodness of his presence made you want to be a better human being. For most of Destiny's adult life, she had to deal with her issues on her own. Besides King, there was no one to talk to. So when Seven came along, he felt like answered prayers.

Seven awakes bright and early. He prays on the side of the bed while watching the virgin sleep. He didn't want to leave her side, but there was work to be done. He catches the city bus to his part of town and was dropped off two miles from the library. He uses the resources available to look up the crime rate in his community. He researched the numbers from three months back and prints out copies. He calls the elementary, Jr. High, and high schools to retrieve the average test scores of the student body as a whole. He took the numbers of the crime rate, the average testing scores for the last three months and entered all the data onto one spreadsheet. He prints out the copies before walking to his apartment. The first thing he does when entering his home was hang up the statistics on his wall. He changes his clothes and fills his backpack up with more books to give away. Before walking out of his apartment, he stared at those numbers on his wall.

When out roaming the community, Seven kept an eye open to ones who were pushing the drugs. He walked the streets at night and looks out his window with a set of binaculars. He kept tabs on their where about's and times they liked to hang outside. He planned to move in at the right time. There were a handful of small time hustler's working for the two main dealers that supplied the area. The two weren't your big time dealers, but they wasn't hurting for any money either. One stood obviously on the block, while the other remained low key. Seven slipped a small note that read, "I would like to present an offer to you, let's talk," along with a $100 bill slightly sticking out of both books. The one dealer who was more low key, just so happened to be leaning up against a Lincoln Town car. Seven began to walk towards him with a few of his health packet books in his hand. The dealer who goes by the name of, "Cash," began to frown as the unfamiliar Seven approaches closer.

SEVEN: How are you doing my brother, I'm just strolling by passing out this book that I believe can help people.

CASH: Thanks but no thanks. I don't need a book.

SEVEN: Not even the money inside? Okay, well you can pass it on to someone if you like. Have a good day.

Seven sat the book down on the ground and walked off while not turning and looking back. He knew that he would eventually run into him again. He just wanted to plant the seed in his mind for now and have him wondering what the offer would be. On to the next dealer was his destination. It was a couple blocks from the apartments where the young hustler named, "Monty," stood outside the corner store. Seven walked inside the store and bought a small bag of unsalted peanuts. He pays for the item and takes out a book with a $100 dollar bill sticking out of it. Also, inside was the note that read, "I want to make you an offer that will be hard to refuse." Seven walks out of the store while pouring peanuts into his mouth. Then he began to approach Monty.

MONTY: Yo who are you?

SEVEN: How you doing my brother?

MONTY: I don't know you to be calling me your brother. So wuz up, you looking for something?

SEVEN: (Pours more peanuts in his mouth while looking into the eyes of Monty) That's understood. Just wanted to give you this book and I'll be on my way.

He hands the book to Monty who could see the money sticking out of the book as he accepts the gift. Seven turns and walks off. Monty opens the book and sees the message next to the money. As Seven continued walking, Monty shouts, "yo come back." Seven stops and turns around as he poured more peanuts inside his mouth. He walks back to being in Monty's vicinity.

MONTY: I don't want to wait. What is this offer you speak of? And wuz up with the money inside, who does that?

SEVEN: I do it, hoping that it grabs your attention.

MONTY: Well you grabbed it, what is this offer you speak of?

Suddenly, Seven changes his positioning when he sees a cop car driving by who happens to be the police officer who wears the eye patch.

MONTY: You scared of the police man?

SEVEN: No, just that one in particular. The cop with the eye patch. What's his deal?

MONTY: I don't know wuz up with that pig. But it's something fishy about him. I always see him rolling around the hood.

SEVEN: You mind if we talk somewhere else other than out in the open?

MONTY: Naw bro, I don't even know you, you can be trying to set me up for all I know. You want to talk, this is my office.

SEVEN: That's respect. So here is the deal. I'll get right to it. What's your price to get you off the block and stop selling to our people?

MONTY: How in the hell you know I'm out here selling?

SEVEN: Word of mouth, and it's not too hard to tell.

MONTY: What, are you the feds?

SEVEN: The feds will have you locked up in prison, I'm here to help prevent that from happening. What, is this it? Is this the life you want, taking a risk every day? What about your future? You can't do this forever. I know there is something else out there you wouldn't mind becoming.

MONTY: (Suspiciously looking) What are you, Malcolm X, Martin Luther King? What do you care what I do? This is how I get it.

SEVEN: Because I want to see us prosper. Because I want kids one day and don't want my teenager to have the option to buy drugs when leaving the corner store. Because I'm tired of seeing us being locked away in prisons. You think God created you to hustle on the streets? Your still young man. You still have a chance.

MONTY: (Contemplating) So what kind of offer you talking about?

SEVEN: Give me a price. What is it going to take?

MONTY: Oh I get it, you want me to stop hustling so you buy me out and take over my customers.

SEVEN: I'm not about selling poison to my people. This here book, this is free essential knowledge, wisdom and good food for the heart, mind and soul. I understand you have to survive and may not want to work for anybody. I feel that, but if you have to bring your people down, in order for you to come up, that's foul. Let's do some math. I'm assuming, let's say you make $500 a day, if that. And let's say you work seven days a week. $500 times 7 days equals $3,500. There are four weeks in a month, so $3,500 times four equals $14,000. I'll give $14,000 to leave this life alone and start a new one for yourself. You could go to trade school, perfect your craft of whatever you have a passion in. Take this money and start your own business. What do you say?

MONTY: $14,000 to stop hustling huh? That sounds too good to be true.

SEVEN: Try me.

MONTY: Man who sent you?

SEVEN: God. How about you think about it (Takes out a pen and reaches for Monty to hand him the book. He writes his phone number on the first page and hands the book back). Go ahead and let this life go before it becomes too late. Hope to talk to you soon. Hopefully we can sit down and talk before I give you the money. Have a blessed day.

He turns around and walks off leaving the young Monty in deep thought. Seven thought to himself, maybe he was offering to much money. But he also knew, Monty was one of the head honchos out here who has many of the small time hustler's working for him. If he could get in good with Monty, that would lead him to the others for way less. If you take Monty out of the equation, then the drugs going out into the community reduces.

On his way home he sees an ice cream truck being chased down by kids. He walked to the truck and speaks to the kids. "Get whatever you would like, I'm buying today." The kid's that were standing at a distance from the ice cream truck were doing so from not having any money. "Kids, yall come over here if you want some ice cream." Around six kid's came running up to the musical truck. Seven shakes the hand of the truck driver while telling the kids to get whatever they liked. One of the kids touched his arm, while the youngest out of the bunch tapped on his leg and making his request. The joy of seeing their faces light up over something so small was priceless.

The dealer named, "Cash," who leaned up against his car witnessed Seven buying ice cream for the Kid's. The kiddos who mismatched freely thanked him. Their pure energy generated boldness to ask without wondering who would disapprove.

SEVEN: Kid's, I want to ask you all a question. How many of you are being raised by your mom. She takes care of you and your brother and sisters by herself?

Seven out of the eleven kid's either raised their hand or responded, "me."

SEVEN: Ok, well after we finish eating our ice cream, I want you take me to your parents.

He followed the kids to their apartment to speak with the single mother. Come to his surprise, two out of those seven single moms were actually their grandmother, and one was a single parent dad. Once they answered the door, he was short of breath. He let it be known that he came in peace. Also, hoping that him buying the kid's ice cream would not be going against their wishes. He handed each parent a book, then asked if he could be a blessing by them writing out a list of things they needed for their household. After collecting all the data from the sixth single guardians, he folded his list up and put it in his pocket. The list was mostly more of the necessities of food and toiletries. A few mentioned how they could use some help on a bill rather than food. So he did indeed. When they all asked his name, he said " just call him brother." There were a few parents who didn't want or need any help, although they accepted the free book.

Seven called up the same Uber driver named Diego for some shopping. Mr. Diego and Seven made a verbal agreement over the phone to be Sevens personal Uber driver. Seven made it clear that he didn't want his business told to anyone. Diego agreed and accepted the offer to have his pay doubled. Diego was a 35 year old Mexican American man who took pride in everything he was apart of. Seven admired his professionalism, consideration, and how clean he kept his car. Diego was a man of a few words. That changed after the fifth day of reading the book given to him. He finally struck up a conversation with Seven who slumped down in the back seat staring out the window.

DIEGO: I want to thank you for the book you gave me my friend.

SEVEN: Your more than welcome my brother.

DIEGO: That is some powerful things you wrote in the book. Enough to cause people to help themselves and not relay on paying all of this money to doctor's.

SEVEN: Wow, just the simple fact that you read the book is awesome. I'm just hoping it can be a blessing to you.

DIEGO: Oh, it has my friend. I applied the information you gave on page 11 you told me to read, and the rash on my arm is almost gone. Not to mention, my blood pressure hasn't been high. I read the book and I tell you Seven, you came right on time.

SEVEN: (Seven rises up from his seat and leans closer towards the front) I'm so thankful to hear that.

DIEGO: I've never been big on religion, or even real spiritual although I believe that Jesus is the son of God, I guess over time of countless hurt, death, and sickness. It just piles up on me and I lose sight for too long. And despite what we are going through, we still have to work to pay the bills. Now you have to have two sources of income just to make it. It drains me. When none of your prayers of healing are being answered, after time, I started to lose faith. But this book here, has caused me to reconnect with God. It brings me hope. Hope that I was losing.

SEVEN: I'm glad the book is able to do so. If you don't mind me asking. When you say, "none of the prayers of healing are not being answered," is there something you are trying to heal?

DIEGO: My wife and I have been married nine years and we haven't been able to have a baby. It's been challenging on us both. It's the main cause of her depression. She feels like something is wrong with her. She wanted to be a mother so bad. I sit there and watch the look on her face at quinceaneras, and I know it hurts her. That smile isn't real. We tried everything the doctors had us do. We tried going to church and the pastor praying over us. We tried everything except having the money to have a procedure done. None of it has worked. So now, we have been trying some of the things you put in your book.

While listening to Diego speak, Seven silently asks God to work through him. He would go on to ask questions such as, what is his wife's diet consist of over the years? How many days out of the week do they eat fast food? What symptoms does she have? What prescription of medicine and vitamins is she taking consistently? Diego answered back honestly while Seven was registering everything in his mind like a doctor.

SEVEN: May I pray with her. All three of us together. Tonight, after I drop off these items to my neighbor's.

DIEGO: You think that will be the key?

SEVEN: If all three of us have 100 percent faith, then of course I do.

DIEGO: I'll call her while you are in the store to see what she thinks.

SEVEN: How about you come inside the store with me, so I can show the food items you should be buying now. And we can talk as well. There are some things I would like to share with you.

DIEGO: Sounds like a plan. I actually think she will be glad to speak with you. She reads the book you gave and is thankful for it. But she has not tried to apply any of the teachings.

The two weaved in and out of aisles while picking up items on the list. Seven took Diego to school on dealing with human body. He gave details on the wonders of how the body is designed to heal itself. He led Diego to the vegan section of the store and recommended food items. He pointed out what to look for on the ingredients and how to know if they are organic or not. School was in session while Seven was filling up his shopping cart. Diego took all the information in, while Seven spoke straight forward and direct from really wanting the information be comprehended. The seeds were planted to better prepare Diego for the guidance of his wife's healing process.

Both men fill the trunk and back seat full of groceries and items needed. The bags were separated according to which household they were assigned to. Diego drives to each apartment where Seven carries the grocery bags to each single parents household. One by one he drops off bags and some cash to pay some bills. When Seven was invited inside each home, he mentally prayed for the holy-spirit to enter the home. He silently prayed for each person he shook hands with. He was casting out spirits and generational curses to leave the home in his mind. He silently prayed for protection, knowledge, wisdom, and understanding while looking into the eyes of the receivers. When Seven was inside one of the homes, Diego called his wife to inform her that he wasn't coming home alone. On the way there, Seven was praying that the holy spirit of God to guide and work through him. He prayed for himself to be cleansed before praying with others. He prayed for God's grace and mercy. He asked God to bless him to be a vessel of healing and he truly believed that he would receive what he was praying for.

Once after Diego introduced his wife to Seven, they would all sit at the dining room table and converse. Without making it look obvious, Seven paid very close attention to her in order to get a better read of his intuition. He feels her energy. He looks into her eyes as she speaks. He watches to see if the edges of her finger tips were jittery. He wanted to see if her skin glowed and how healthy her hair looked. He took in all of what he received and then calculated everything together.

• • •

Then aligned it all up with the knowledge and wisdom he gained in the realm of self-healing..

SEVEN: According to what information you two have shared with me, you have never detoxed your body. Meaning, over the years of consuming of the toxins, processed foods, and GMO's that still resides in the body. Even if it is a micro amount of it, over the years it causes a buildup, leading the body in an acidic state which may affect the process of getting pregnant. The stress can only hurt the situation. Stress can intensify anything that is wrong inside the body. The body follows the mind. So what we need to do is try and eliminate the stress as much as possible. Instead, start believing that you can and will produce a baby. Start believing. Start speaking it out loud so you will be speaking it into existence. And while you are cleansing your body, your thoughts can be manifesting itself.

Your diet will be the most important factor to healing. Let's take out fast foods, meat and dairy while on this mission. It's time to eat more live foods that come from the earth. Take on the mindset that you are eating to heal and feel good again. Eliminate what all you read on the internet of how your chances of getting pregnant are slim. None of that matters now. We want all positive thoughts. You have to change your thinking, which more than likely will be the deciding factor. You have to fill your mind with full faith and believe that you can and will have a baby of your own.

In the book of Matthew 18: 20, it reads, "for where two or three gather in my name, there am I with them." So

God is with us and will hear our prayers and will answer our prayers. The key is for all of us to have 100 percent faith and trust in God. We are going to already give thanks in advance. Any doubt can defeat the purpose. So let's all hold hands and pray. All three holds hands while Seven prays. Chill bumps ran through the wife of Diego. A graceful energy electrified the air after the prayer. A sense of hope caused for a smile on the couples face. Seven thought it would be best if he walked the four miles home so Diego and his wife could be together. Diego insisted that he took him home but Seven didn't take no for an answer. He was actually looking forward to his journey home.

Seven puts on his headphones and begins to walk in the midnight hour. The closer he made it to his side of town, the less appealing the city began to look. There seemed to be less street lights and more police cars riding around. The stroll of the police car was more creepy like. The look in their eyes, the energy and vibe came off as if the police were against the people, rather than for us. As if the people here in our own streets of America were terrorist. Seven wondered in his thoughts as he walks fearlessly through the rough streets that never seem to sleep. The death of King pressed an extra dose of boldness to the spirit of Seven. The silent hurt caused him to smile less throughout his day. The feeling he carried in his heart caused him to think of how so many people in the community could be sharing the same hurt. From losing a family member to violence, or having a loved one locked away behind bars. All of the combined hurt and frustration built inside can eventually turn to anger and rebellion. Seven could sense both emotions in a good deal of the young men standing on the street corners. He could sense the lack of fear from the young men as well. The same lack of fear that Seven possessed when walking in an area that most people would avoid.

Seven stops walking in his tracks and just looks at the world around him. He asked himself the questions, how big would I think, after being accustomed to subconsciously seeing and living in the less appealing part of the city most of my life? From the run down school buildings, to the low income apartments that could use some fixing up. Not to mention the number of unhealthy fast food options to choose from. There were thousands of young people and a handful of decent paying jobs to apply. What is the effect of witnessing to your people being taking away in police cars to spend years in prison? How does the police brutality effect the confidence of feeling protected by the ones who are working to serve and protect? What is the root problem to all of the madness? How did the drugs even get into the community in the first place? What is wrong with the criminal justice system? Why can't there be more money put into revamping the community?

The more Seven asked himself questions, the more cause and effect options appeared in an imaginary upwards bubble from where he stood. His understanding was increasing as he connected the dots and filled in the blanks. Despite the odds, there was nothing that was going to break the spirit of Gods people but it didn't have to be like this. Compared to where Seven grew up, to now living in the hood, it seemed like the results of a classified experiment. Could it be called the projects, because it was actually a project once upon a time? It was apparent that more must be done. The problem was deeper than how he was going about making a difference. The note that King left inside the bag full of money kept popping up in his mind. Seven knew that he was going to have to come up with a mastermind game plan in order to bring about a real change.

Seven snaps out of his daydream and carries on to his destination. When walking north on the sidewalk, he spots out a police car driving south. The eye patch wearing police officer was spotted out once again. Seven avoided his face being seen by acting as if he was looking down at his phone. He continues to walk calm once the police car passes by. Once he turns around to look back, the police car begins to make a U turn and drive back towards Seven. He momentarily was stuck, thinking if he should take off running or not. He briefly closes his eyes and asks God to cover him. The police sirens loudly sing it's song. Seven opens his eyes to see the red and blue lights surround the area. He kept walking while his heart raced in his chest. The loud sirens approached closer and closer. Just as the police car moved towards Seven, it picks up speed and passes by and drives off. A side of relief for the midnight walker.

Chapter

12

THE UNDERGROUND APARTMENT

S even moved like an angel in the night. The man on a mission searched for souls in need, while performing walk by blessings throughout the neighborhood. Random strangers were hit with a memory that would last forever. His intuition was telling him that the word was spreading, but to who was the question? The more days that went by, the more he felt like he was being watched. Telling himself that he was just being paranoid didn't help the strong feel to go away. The thought of being watched, and constantly thinking of ways to better the world around him sparked an idea to expand his operation.

Seven was thinking of renting out a second apartment in the same apartments. A three bedroom that would consist of a learning center and health clinic. He was thinking about an underground railroad type of fashion. He thought of ideas such as, holding secret meetings to teach about nutrition, the human body and life coaching. A group think tank. A place where one can go and have their voice heard. A place where you can go and pray together. A place where one can go to build, grow, and gain wisdom.

The apartment would need structure from a set of rules. The organization would need to be enforced in order to maintaining a beneficial system. He would need help to operate the underground apartment. A full-time helper and cook. Both would have to genuinely be down with the movement. That is when Squint came to mind. Not only could Squint help out with the ones who battle addiction, but share his testimonies with the youth as well. The foundation would be built on trust, love, loyalty, and respect.

Seven was thinking of a three bedroom apartment. One being set up like a clinic for health and medical attention. He will able to check blood pressure and cholesterol levels. A degreeless doctor ready to give free medical advice. The second room would turn into a learning center. He would order many powerful books. Readings on the mind, body, spirit, wisdom, history, autobiographies, and handpicked novels. There would be two computers with wifi available. An available chess board and pieces set up. Influential quotes scattered throughout the walls of the room. The third would be set up like a hotel room with two beds. He never knew who may need a place to sleep for the night.

● ● ●

Seven decided to hire a woman from the apartments to be the cook. A few days out of the week would be planned to help feed the homeless, provide healthy school lunches for the kids, and at selective meetings were being held. The rules of the underground apartment were simple, but very important to be applied. The home was open to all, but only by referral, appointment or invite. There were rules and regulations when coming to pay a visit. A visitor must only knock on the door four times exactly, or, when being asked, "who is it," the response must be, "I am your brother." Mostly all visitors would enter from the back door to avoid the obvious traffic. The teen hooper's would have to have their parent's permission to be inside.

Seven wasted no time by putting his plans into action. He used his resources within the apartment by finding the right woman to rent out an apartment in her name. He ordered all that he invisioned inside the apartment ahead of time. Less than 48 hours the apartment was set up just how he imagined it. His thoughts, plans, and vision were in motion. He was in rhythm like a hot shooter on the basketball court. The chips began to fall into the right place. The more books being given out, the more people began to walk up and shake his hand. The essential seeds inside the book were benefiting more and more souls. There were less people going without. Less lights were being turned off. Less people were hanging out outside in the late night hour. There was less drama going on in the neighborhood.

The plan was to end the mission by the end of the summer. Until then, he would activate the love in his heart and make the lives around him better. He had every move mapped out. Every scenario was well thought out and covered. The operation was being designed to continue on without him. He schooled, taught, and trained Squint and Miss Sharon during the journey. Miss Sharon and Seven became closer friends as the time traveled. They both admired each other's soul. A sweetheart indeed, but yet firm. Not only was she just the cook, she was the mother of the home. The elder woman who schooled the young women with food for thought. She gave cooking lessons to the young women at certain meetings, while feeding game on relationship, the power of sex, and understanding their worth.

The only time Seven wanted the word to spread was about the apartment cookout. Although making it clear that he wanted everyone to show up at the start time, he didn't want anybody to show up early to avoid attention from the authorities. Unfortunately, when a large group of black people come together in a lower class community, the gathering is usually shut down or broken up by the police, even if the large crowd was peaceful. Seven didn't want to give the city, or management of the apartment a chance to cancel, or not approve of the special occasion. The plan was to keep the the big cookout amongst the people of the community. Just bring you, the family, and everything else will be provided.

When seven was not out playing the role of an angel in the flesh, he was still working at the library to counter any suspicion. He wanted a paper trail to camouflage the increase of his purchasing. He spent his free time with Destiny June who was slowly but surely recovering from the loss of King. Seven could feel her pain when looking through her eyes. She cried herself to sleep in his arms one night. She would breakdown at random moments of the day. His shoulder was the only one she could lean on. His love for her grew by the day. Destiny was battling the thought of never being the same. Seven was her balance and strength during the worst time of her life. She wanted to be in his presence all the time, but she understood when a man was on a mission. The two texted throughout the day like best friends who were falling in love. He would text her a small piece of poetry and she would respond back with poetry of her own. They went back and forth until they both could feel when to stop.

Seven walks to the basketball court inside the apartment complex. The young hooper's stopped their game once recognizing him. Seven had to mentally gather himself from not crying when seeing how happy the teenagers were to see him. They dapped, man hugged, and shook hands. They all moved to the bench area where they gathered around. The basketball stopped bouncing and their undivided attention was on Seven.

SEVEN: What's going on my young kings? I would like to propose an opportunity to make some money. Now some of you may already have one, but I say we meet up right here tomorrow and we all walk to the library. If you don't have one, it's time to get a library card. I will show you how to search for books on the computer. It is key that you all read. Knowledge can be power. So here is how you earn your money. For every book you read, I give you 50 dollars cash. Once you finished reading the book, you have to write me a one page summary of the book you read. There is no limit of how much money you can earn. Let's do some math. Let's say you read 2 books a week. That is 100 dollars. There are 4 weeks in a month. So 100 dollars times 4, equals to 400 dollars you made in 1 month.

That is the first way you can earn some money. The second option is, we meet up once a week and go around to pick up trash. All over the whole complex and around the community. This is where you live. This is your neighborhood. So we must take care of it. It may not seem like much right now, but if God can trust you with a little, he will be able to trust with a lot. I will pay you 25 dollars each. Now, for the third and final opportunity for you to earn some money. When your last report cards come out, if you pass with A's or B's and no C's, for every A you get, I give you 50 dollars. And for every B you get, I give you 25 dollars. Another thing I wanted to tell you young kings... I rented out a new apartment that is meant for mind elevation and building. And with your parent's permission, this apartment will be open to you guys. We can meet up 1 or 2 days out of the week if you like. This is where we will conduct our business if you decide to earn some money. There will be days where you can come and just hang out. We can watch the game, talk about life, learn new things, discuss books, watch documentaries, and have bible studies. So what do you say?

Seven leaves the group of young men momentarily speechless. A few were soaking it all in, while others where smiling from the good news. One of the youngsters gave Seven a man hug. "Thank you Mr., because Lord knows, this opportunity came right on time." "It sho did," as the tallest player on the team spoke out. Some of the teens were mentally doing the math in their mind, while others began asking questions. "When can we start coming over to the apartment, I'm ready to start building?" "Yea, me too, when is the first session?" "We can discuss that after our first gathering at the library," Seven replied. Cool, they replied at once. The smallest player on the team stuck out his hand towards Seven and asks, "why are you doing all of this for us?" "Because, I am your brother," Seven replies.

The priceless faces of the young men kept Seven up throughout the night. He sat by the window for a long period of time and stared out his project window. He has become closer with the beautiful souls of the neighborhood outside his home. To his surprise, the drug dealer Monty calls to discuss the deal. Seven knew he had him then. Now it was just about getting Monty to see his vision. The two spoke and set up a time and date for the meeting. Seven requested that Monty brought his hustler's that worked for him. He was skeptical at first about allowing these men to come inside the underground apartment, but he wanted them to see how passionate he was about cleaning the streets up. He wanted them to feel him when he spoke his vision for the community. He wanted to show his love and hospitality by having Miss Sharon cook a meal that would be prepared on the dinner table.

The two men spoke and set up a time and date. The very next day, the first meeting at the underground think tank was held. Monty accepted the request and brought his young hustler's to the meeting. A party of five sitting at one table. Salad, grilled chicken, fish, sweet yams, collard greens, cornbread, and macaroni and cheese placed out on the table. Seven got to know each individual before making his offer. Between the positive vibes, good eating, and his genuine will to give back had the group of young men tuned in. When first entering the apartment you could feel their guards being up. It wasn't long before they felt like they were at home.

Seven has already given Monty a price to stop selling drugs, now he was working on Monty's foot soldiers. He made them an offer to stop selling drugs. And if they were willing to do so, he was going to either help lead them to find a job, get enrolled into a trade school or college. He offered to give them his personal phone number if they ever needed some advice, guidance, someone to talk to, or to pray with. In the midst of his generosity, Seven spoke with authority and passion. By the end of the night, the young hustlers were all aboard to making the positive change.

Although Seven had more money, he still had to play chess. He pretends to make a call to someone who was on their way with the money. He did not want anyone to believe that he kept large amounts of money inside the underground apartment. Seven allowed 15 minutes to pass, he stepped outside for a quick minute and came back inside with the offer money. Seven walks back inside, takes out the money, and places it on the table.

SEVEN: A friend of mine blessed me with some money to put back into the community. And this is it right here. The rest is to keep this apartment running. This is how for real I am to help clean up this area. It is my pleasure to give you this money for the start of a new beginning. I'm proud of you king's accepting my offer. Now I must say, if you receive this money, and get caught on the block hustling, my unknown guy who just dropped off this money will come see you. And he won't be coming to talk. Do we have that understood, are we all on the same page my brothers? (The understanding was so by the group of men)

One person with health needs would come to visit Seven's clinical room and would tell a friend. That friend would come and eventually tell a friend. Before Seven knew it, he was playing the role of an underground doctor. He gave out natural herbs for free. He wrote out diet plans. He gave out his health packet books. He taught meditation techniques for self- healing. His patient's were coming back with positive results. The word spread like a silent outbreak. It got to a point where he eventually had schedule appointments. He still met up with the group of young hooper's twice a week. One meeting for a building sessions, and the other was to give the money they earned. He spoke on the importance of how they treated the woman. The importance of setting goals, staying focused, perfecting their craft, using their body as a temple and seeking knowledge. He also made the young men take out the time to write their loved ones who were locked away in prison.

Seven would hold dinners for a few battling addictions. Squint would share his testimonies, while naturally providing laughter for the soul. The underground apartment that provided free health care, free counseling, fellowship, and a free meal was quietly becoming powerful. They would go running together. One night he would teach a class on how to write poetry. There were a few saturday's where he and Destiny June would rent a small bus and take field trips with the youth. They visited places like the museum, a musical symphony and to ride horses. He wanted the youngster's to experience things they were not exposed to. Destiny would speak to the young women on conducting themselves like ladies. She would teach about understanding your worth as a woman. She spoke about sex, absinence, women's health and the risks of being on birth control.

While things were going smooth, in the back of Seven's mind, he knew it was only a matter of time before the underground apartment didn't become so underground. So far there was no sign of the cop with the eye patch or the North side boys looking for him. Until that time came, he remained optimistic about properly running his operation. With that being said, it costs money to run the underground apartment and the money was being spent fast. Soon as he began to think of ways to make the money last, the feel it gave of helping someone was a feel like no other. The expression on a mother's face when making her day. The handshake and look in the mans eyes when helping with a little extra to get over financial hump. The joy in the teens eyes when having snack money for the rest of the week. The priceless moment of young man turn from the street life and want to change for the good. The happiness it brought to know people appreciated his existence. From walking down the street and people being glad to see him, to random people sharing their testimonies after reading his health book. His favorite expression by stranger he gave to was, "you came at the right time," which let him know that God was working through him.

The night before the big cookout, Miss Sharon, Squint and Seven sat around the table and discussed plans. Right before their conversing was coming to an end, there was a unusual knock on the front door, knock.. knock.. knock.. knock.. knock. Once the fifth knock was heard, the three looked at each other with a look of concern. "That was five knocks, the code is four,"

Squint speaks curiously. Seven puts his finger over his lips to inform the others to be quiet. He quietly walks to the front door. Right before he slowly looks into the peep hole, knock.. knock.. knock.. knock.. knock. Disappointment arose on the face of Seven when looking through the peep hole and seeing the police officer with the eye patch standing at the door. His one eye pierced back into the peep hole. Seven took a step back and shook his head from knowing he's got a problem on his hands. Seven walks towards the table and informs Miss Sharon to stay calm and answer all his questions that they had prepared for. Seven made sure his people were well prepared for all situations that could possibly come about.

All three looked at the front door when hearing tapping on the door. The officer began lightly tapping with the knuckle of his middle finger, knock.. knock.. knock.. knock.. knock.. An eerie energy came about when hearing the the same repetitive knocks. The cop said nothing while standing in silence. The three sat at the table wondering if the cop had left or not. Then BOOM!! He pounds the door with the side of his balled fist, causing Miss Sharon to jump. Squint puts his arm around Miss Sharon and tells her that it's going to be okay. The officer leaves from the front door. Seven stood there in thought, he didn't want to face the blues, but he knew right then and there that he was being watched.

All three remained silent. Suddenly, they hear from the back door, knock.. knock.. knock.. knock.. knock.. This time Squint jumps from being frightened. Miss Sharon puts her arm around Squint and tells him that it's going to be okay. Squint played it off as if he didn't get scared. Seven would have laughed, but now was not the time. The officer began to whistle a tune, while waiting to see if someone was going to open the door. Then once again, knock.. knock.. knock.. knock.. knock.. was the sound from the side window. The officer carried on, whistling until his next stop, knock.. knock.. knock.. knock.. knock.. now coming from the living room window. They watched the police officer's shadow from the outside. The officer began to whistle again, while slowly walking back to the front door. Knock.. knock.. knock.. knock. knock.. He finally speaks, "we need to talk," loud enough to be heard. While walking away from the door, the officer begins to sing, "oh Destiny, where art thou Destiny, ohh Destiny, where art thou Destiny," in a Frank Sinatra tone of voice. His voice slowly went down the further he walked away. Seven's fearless demeanor weakened when hearing Destiny's name. He immediately called her and told her to leave.

Miss Sharon let Seven use her car. He would stay on the phone with Destiny until she was by his side. Seven knew the originally planned date to hand over the operation would have to come sooner. He was not aware of what the officer knew, or what he was after. The only thing that mattered right now was seeing Destiny. Once the two met at the half way point, she could feel something was wrong.

DESTINY: What happen?

SEVEN: The same police officer I ran into at the emergency room came to the apartment tonight. I didn't open the door. He said we needed to talk, then he mentioned your name as if he was coming to look for you.

DESTINY: The same officer we dodged, the one who was standing outside near your apartment?

SEVEN: Yes, the one with the eye patch. But this time he went to the underground apartment.

DESTINY: I wonder if they have been investigating us. I mean, King was a ghost up until he left us, and you are making a difference in the neighborhood. Seven let's leave. Let's leave right now. Let's get out of here. Your work is done here. I've never been without my brother King like this and I don't know what I will do if I lose you too.

SEVEN: Okay. I'm with it.

DESTINY: I mean right now Seven.

SEVEN: It pains to me to say this.. but D, I really need to be a part of this event in the afternoon. I need to do this for my own peace the rest of the way. I made a promise and must keep it.

DESTINY: (Swallowed her pride and tried to be understanding) I don't have a good feeling but I trust you. I always have since the day you saved me. (Comes into the arms of Seven)

SEVEN: Let's go check into a room for the night. Don't worry about anything. I will go get things setup and visit for a minute. I won't stay the whole time. Then we can leave and go be free. Were you want to go? I don't even have to know. It can be in the worst part of the world and that would be fine with me. As long as I am with you, I'm good.

DESTINY: I already have the location setup.

SEVEN: Oh you do.

DESTINY: Yes, it's perfect for just me and you. I want it to be a surprise. I know you'll love it.

The two leave and check into a room for the night. Seven massaged Destiny to sleep while he wondered, thought and prayed. He understood the chance he was taking by being at the family cookout but he was all in. Despite the pressure, he moved fearlessly as King would. One more task before moving away with the woman who stayed on his mind from the moment he laid eyes on her. He was fascinated how the virgin moved through life. She was the movie, a walking piece of art. Destiny June, away from the many disguises, all there by his side.

Seven awoke at sun rise. He leaves the queen in her dreams and met the workers to help set up the cookout event. He paid to have the caterer's serve the food. He and the workers set up the bounce house, tables, and games for the kids. He brought out his DJ equipment from his one bed room apartment and set it up. The referee crew to officiate the basketball tournament were present. The shot clock and scoreboard were set up and ready for the games to begin. Besides the people who were helping set up the event, the people were yet to arrive, just as planned.

Right when 12 o'clock hit, the people came out of their apartments and cars began to pull up at once. Familiar faces of the neighborhood arrived one after another. Mothers, fathers, aunts, uncles, cousin, grandmothers, grandfathers and friends began to fill the whole open area by the basketball court. You could feel a positive vibe in the air. The looks on the peoples face were priceless. Seven had to hold in his tears throughout the cookout, despite knowing the cop with the eye patch could show up at any time. He wished King could have witnessed the smile on Squints face as he ran the carnival booths. Seeing the kids run around and playing. The adults sat in lawn chairs and enjoyed watching the celebration. The slamming of dominoes and friendly trash talking from the domino tournament taking place. The young group of hustlers who stopped selling were there enjoying themselves. Some people danced to the music that Seven DJ'd. The young hooper's were all balling on the basketball court while many people watched them do there thing. There was enough food to go around. Smiles upon smiles, laughter, good vibes, good music, and no drama. Seven dreamed of wanting to DJ events and never have until this very moment.

One by one, a great deal of the crowd would walk up to Seven and show their love and appreciation. It was the first time seeing Seven in person for most people. They only heard of the mystery man by word of mouth. He gained the respect of famous drug dealers from the neighborhood, but only he was dealing love, hope, and change. He was spreading love while heightening the awareness of the people. People were just wanting to shake his hand, hug him, and take pictures with him. The elders showed their appreciation to the young Seven who played good songs one after another. Joy came over him when seeing Diego and his wife together. They approached him and both hugged him. Diego was smiling from ear to ear when his wife gave Seven a thank you card. When Seven opened the card, there was a picture inside of a pregnancy test with two lines, which meant she was finally going to have her first baby. All three hugged each other in the priceless moment.

Seven kept checking the time to know when to leave to meet Destiny at the bus stop. He had a little time left to stay and visit. He never was one to speak in front of a crowd, but it was heavy on his heart to do so. He didn't want to leave town without giving a proper exit. There was a bittersweet feel in doing so, but he got out of his comfort zone and grabbed the microphone from his DJ set. He took a step up on the bench seat to where the crowd could see him.

SEVEN: Good day my brothers and sisters. (The crowd stopped what they were doing and gave seven their undivided attention) I have always been too nervous to talk in front of a crowd, but I see you all as my family, so I don't feel that way right now. I'm not going to be long, I just want to tell you something (long pause while gathering his thoughts). I would like for you all to do something for me. Turn to the left and turn to the right. You see those people to your left and right? We have to start seeing them as your family. You don't have to be friends or hang out, but what I'm saying is, we have to adopt the mindset that we are family, and we are all in this thing together. Meaning, we have to get back to the saying, it takes a village to raise a home. If you look out and see the next man as your brother, you will be less prone to hate on them, to lie, steal, cheat, and destroy them. We have to look at that kid who isn't yours and see that kid as being connected to you. Young men, don't be deceived by how the entertainment world portrays our sisters. We have to look at our women as being queens. None of us would be here without the woman. She is the carrier of us, she is connected to the earth and universe. She needs to be in a healthy state of mind and stress free when carrying our seeds. Anything less than wanting to treat women with respect, love, and protect her even if she isn't your wife, is like going against the laws of nature, and it's almost like having a sick mentality. A mind deceived by the world.

In the book of Romans 12:2 "it says, Do not be conformed to this world, but be transformed by the renewing of your mind, that you may prove what is that good and acceptable and perfect will of God." Young ladies. Don't spend the same amount of time in the mirror as you do with the time you put in the advancement of your mind. You are beautiful the way God made you. Discover who you are as a woman and understand your worth here on earth. Do not settle for anything. Respect your brother. Start to believe in the man. Be each other's rock. Men lift the woman up, and woman lift the man up. And together we can create a better frequency between the two. Form a contagious energy that spreads and can only produce goodness.

Elders, you all have been there and done it all. You all have keys that we younger generation need. Feed us the game, help prepare the generation below. We all have to feed and get the minds of our children right, for they are the future. We need to straighten up when we are around kids because they are like sponges. From watching our actions and listening to the words we speak. We must protect them from the evil ways of the world. Learn about spiritual warfare, that is what we are all up against whether we know or not. Well, now is the time. Now is the time to gain knowledge and wisdom if you lack it, for in the bible it reads in Hosea 4:6, "My people are destroyed for a lack of knowledge." A lot of us are battling illnesses, stress, worry, and fear that stems from a lack of knowledge. It's time to start monitoring our diet better and know what we are putting in our body.

(In the middle of speaking to the crowd of people, Seven sees the big husky north side guy towards the back who began making his way towards the front. Seven pauses for a moment and looks at Monty who was standing near Seven. Monty immediately felt that

Seven had seen something in the crowd that caused him to pause. Monty looks into the crowd from where he was standing. Seven would hear voices in the crowd shout, "speak on it my brother, yes that's what I'm talking about, and preach!)

SEVEN: (Speeds up his speech with passion) Protect your mind. That is what the enemy is after. That is where it all starts. Believe in yourself. Everyone look at your fingertips right now. You see that fingerprint of yours? You are the only person in the whole wide world who has that fingerprint. That is your power. You are here for a reason. You are one of a kind family, use it to your advantage. Don't ever try to be like somebody else. I'm not preaching, nor teaching, I just love you all. I wish you all a prosperous and healthy life. I am your brother.

Seven steps down from the bench. he whole crowd clapped and cheered. The big north side guy weaved through the crowd getting closer to Seven. Seven stepped in towards Squint, "I will be in contact with you, everything that you see of mine is now yours my brother, I have to leave now, "I'm proud of you, and hugged Squint. Seven tried to walk away but the crowd closed closer to him. Seven nervously shook hands while lifting his head to see where the north side guy was approaching from. Right when the big guy muscled his way out from the crowd within arm's reach, is when the two of Monty's boys jumped right in front of him. Before the north side guy knew it, he was surrounded by a few more goons who were ready for problems.

I Am Your Brother

Monty pointed up to another man near the surrounded Seven. That is when the two men lifted Seven on their shoulders. Seven arose higher to the sky and could see the top of a crowd of cheering people. Seven could see how the north side guy was backing away after being confronted. They began to walk with Seven on their shoulders away from the north side guy. The most gratifying feeling that Seven has ever experienced was happening. The group of people below the elevated Seven began to chant, "I AM YOUR BROTHER, HEYYYY! I AM YOUR BROTHER, HEYYYY! I AM YOUR BROTHER HEYYYY! A priceless feel of energy that caused chill bumps throughout his body . He looked up to the sky and thanked God. "So this is what King felt when he was being carried high in the air for doing a good deed." Pure joy from the smiling Seven.

Monty and the other man carrying Seven let him down. Seven shakes Monty's hand and thanks him before he took off running. The crowd was still chanting, while the few who knew his plans waved bye. He ran to the car he came in, opens the trunk, and takes out the black backpack before hurrying into the driver's seat. He put the keys in the ignition and took off towards Destiny who awaited his arrival. Seven couldn't believe it. Everything he planned was happening right before his eyes. It was all happening. It wasn't even a mile from the apartments while sitting at a red light and a Lincoln Town car pulls up next to him. Seven looks to his left and sees that Cash was the driver. The main drug supplier of the apartments, the only one that refused the book and chose not to hear the offer.

Before the light turned green, the two just stared at each other before Cash signaled Seven to roll his window down. When Seven rolled his window down, Cash raised a pistol towards the face of Seven. "Pull over right now before I put holes in your face," Cash speaks aggressively. Seven froze with his hands up. "Put your hands down and pull over to the side right there," Cash yells from the other car. "This can't be happening right now," Seven thought to himself. All he could think about was getting to Destiny. He thought about driving off before Cash yelled, "pull over right now before I let this thing loose!" Seven fought to fight another day and did as he was told.

Seven pulled over on the side of the street and Cash parked right behind him. He then sees police lights in his rear view mirror. A cop car pulled up and parked behind Cash. A side of relief from Seven, thinking the cop was there for his rescue. While staring through the rear view mirror, he could see a policeman get out of his car. It just so happened to be the cop with the eye patch. Seven couldn't believe what he was seeing. The cop walked up to the side door of the Lincoln and he and Cash shook hands. Cash began to slowly drive off while looking at Seven as he passes by. Seven looked back at the rear view mirror to see the cop just standing there looking towards him. Then it all came to Seven. That was why Cash wanted no parts of him or the deal. He was working with the cop, paying the cop in order to sell his drugs, and not be bothered with.

The cop began to walk towards the front door of Seven. He approached the door while still facing forward. Then slowly looked down at Seven. He takes the knuckle of his middle finger and taps on the window, knock.. knock.. knock.. knock.. knock. Seven rolls his window down and looks at the one eye that stares back. The two just stare at each other before speaking.

Chapter 13

THE SACRIFICE

O FFICER: You almost made it to her.

SEVEN: How did you know that?

OFFICER: Your willingness to care. An undercover who needed some clinical assistance. We need to talk. Get out the car.

SEVEN: I can't do that officer, not today. I have somewhere I need to be. Besides, I know my rights.

As Seven began to recite the rights that pertained to him, the officer looked to his left and right to see if any cars were driving by. He pulls out his gun and presses the barrel on Seven's neck. "Do as I say boy, or else your road stops here," the officer speaks. "And bring that backpack with you." Seven reaches over and grabs the bag before slowly getting out of the car. The officer puts his gun back in his holster and took out his handcuffs. The cars passing by slowed down to a nosy speed. He walks Seven to the police car and assists him into the back seat. He closes the door and steps inside the driver seat. The officer checks to make sure the camera remained off. He then turns around and stares at Seven through the clear shield that divides them.

OFFICER: Well, well, well.. we cross paths once again. And there goes that same black backpack you wore on that very night. Perhaps, handed down from the infamous King. The one who has robbed nearly half of the dealers out here. One being the Northside boys. I guess you could say, who I have a little partnership with. And your friend robbed one of the Northside boys for a pretty good penny and a part of that money just so happened to be mine. Which makes it my business. And just when I thought they got rid of the King here comes his clever sidekick. I've been putting it all together, going into a great deal of research on you and King. And I must admit, you guys are good. I'm willing to bet you took a great deal of that money and used it to clean up these streets. How heroic of you. I'm debating if I should get your autograph, or maybe a selfie, just to let the people know that I met the guy before he was no more. That is if, I get my money back. (Turns back around and drives off) Oh, my apologies, I happen to be officer Romanowski. And you have the right to remain silent, anything you say, can and will be held against you in a court of law. No.. I am the law today. I'm an eye for an eye type of guy. (Looks at Seven with his one eye through the rear view mirror) You know what I mean.. and who might the ghost man's name be?

SEVEN: My name is Seven.. and I ran out of money.

OFFICER: (Long pause before taking out his baton and lying it across the passenger seat) Well, that's just too bad.

The officer's phone rang and he didn't bother to not take the call off speaker phone. "Did you get him?" "Yes, I have him in my possession as we speak, thanks to Cash," the officer replied. Seven could recognize the voice on the speaker. He realized it from the time he was in the bathroom stall on the night he first met Destiny. Then it all came to him. It was indeed the big husky guy from the Northside on the phone. Officer Romanowski was being paid from both Cash and the Northside boys to allow them to hustle without being messed with.

Seven noticed they were driving further away from the police station when seeing this red, white, and blue painted stand that sold fireworks for the 4th of July. He didn't have a good feeling about the intentions of the officer, not to mention him feeling sick about not being with Destiny right now. He could feel his phone vibrate inside his pocket nonstop. It was mental torcher from knowing it's Destiny wondering where he was at. He totally regretted not making Destiny tell him where she planned on moving to. His only way to get of hold of her was by phone. He had to think fast on how he could escape. His mind raced with options. Why would a cop

● ● ●

keep him alive to tell his story of the corruption. Or could the cop be driving towards the North so the Northside boys could finish him off. Or what did he plan on doing with his baton out. Despite the nightmarish situation, his only option were to lean towards his faith and trust that God would see him through.

OFFICER: All you had to do is take the money and get lost. Move out of the ghetto and go on a vacation. But no, you had to go clean up the streets and give back to people who has never did anything for you. Not realizing that you were hurting my business. Less drug dealers to lock up. Less prostitutes walking around leading me to who is doing what. Less action out here in the streets you know. Less of a war zone. So just recently, I was in a meeting full of police officer's. And the sergeant says out loud, "whatever officer Romanowski is doing out in the Sunset Terrace area, it is working." Then he pulls up statistics so he could compare last year to the first half of this year. And the crime rate has dropped drastically each month. They are hardly getting any calls from the schools in the area for violence. As matter of fact, each school from the elementary, Jr. high and high schools, all three of the schools grade point average has increased ten points. Each month the grade point average increased. I even hear the doctors in this area are seeing less and less patients come in for checkups. And I get a good deal of the credit for having a helping hand in the crime rate going down. Little do they all know, it was one man orchestrating this whole thing out, and he was nowhere to be found.

The more I did my undercover work, I began to discover more and more. But he was good, somehow he got so many people who knew, but did not spill the beans. From that moment on, I knew I was going to have to play rough, because it was bigger than money with this ghost I was looking for. He was winning the people's heart, which comes the real power. I had to prey on the weak, and threaten a couple drug addicts, fix them up a little, slap them around a little until they spoke. I threatened to take people to jail. I started asking around, putting that deadly eye on them, and intimidating. Coming to lie, steal, cheat and destroy, until I find this hero. And they began to speak and tell me what I needed to hear. You should have seen their eyes after talking. Poor things, they looked so sad. And I'll have you know, once I knew who the ghost was, and your whereabouts it got strange. The oh so many times I had you right at my finger tips, with my eye on you, and for the first time before being conditioned, I started to wonder if there was a God, because you just seem to slip through my fingertips somehow, some way, without even knowing I was on your tail. And so, after I received my little award plague for doing such fine work in the community, I got after you boy. I became obsessed with you. I thought about you more than my wife. Cause you were really starting to hurt my business. The other ghost, King, put so much fear in a lot of these drug dealers who paid me a percentage. I relied on these dealers, junkies, and these worthless humans who were just taking up space. I needed to catch you and make you pay. I believe in your bible it reads, "seek and you shall find." And I finally found you. And so I have something for you to see (holds up the award plague with one hand and steering the wheel with the other) Isn't that something?

SEVEN: I think it's a shame.

OFFICER: (Looking at Seven through the rear view mirror) How so?

SEVEN: It's a shame how one man, with a little money can do to help make a big difference in a community in so little time. And our American government who spends millions a day to fund war. Our group of intelligence have yet to put together an intelligent game plan to improve the lower income communities all across America. All these people with degree's and making big decisions have yet to come up with a game plan to bring about real change. They have yet to figure it out. When really, there is not much to figure out. You just have to have the right kind of heart to do it. One who possesses true love in his heart, one who is not about greed, or driven by the force of pride, control and power. It takes one who has God in their heart and genuinely wants the best for all the people of this country.

OFFICER: (Slowly begins to clap his hands with a grin on his face) Bravo, and the Oscar for best drama goes too, Seven. The one on the run, on a path to glory, nowhere to be found. Unfortunately, no one cares. It's a game out here, and if you don't play the game, the game will play you.

SEVEN: (Scoots up to the edge of his seat to where his face was just inches from the clear shield) I understand officer Romanowski. I understand your pain. This world has turned you heartless. On top of that being a police officer. I bet you have seen all the crazy things this world has to offer. You get to see the worst part of us people. You see death, you see people killing each other, rapist, men sexually abusing kids, having to lock people up, corruption, and strife in this rat race. You witness all that on top of your own personal fight. On top of not having God in your heart. That has to be a lot on you officer Romonowski.

OFFICER: Lean back in your seat boy.

SEVEN: Oh trust me, I understand. I'm praying for you officer. I pray that God touches you like never before, and may Gods will be done.

OFFICER: Oh, he's good everyone! (He shouts while he stares at Seven through his rear view mirror) Will see where your God is at here shortly.

SEVEN: God, touch this man, come into his heart and have him turn from his wicked way. In the name of Jesus I pray.

OFFICER: Sit back and shut your mouth with all this God shit.

SEVEN: (Moves back in his seat) Cover this man dear Lord. May the Holy Spirit touch his mind.

The officer made an exit from the highway and turned on the next available road. A road that lead closer to an area with a lot of trees. Seven realized the turn off was not where the officer attended to drive. Seven could feel that he struck a nerve to where he made his matters worse. He could sense the officers blood boiling, covered by his solid and evil eye. Seven prepared in his mind for the worse, although not losing one bit of faith. The officer pulled in an area where no one could see them and parked the car. He turned off the engine and lit a cigar. He got out of the car and walked around to the passenger side door and leaned back up against the car. He stared straight while puffing his cigar. He took one last puff and burned it out on the ground. He opened the passenger door and placed his cigar in the ash tray before grabbing his baton. His one eye stared at Seven from the outside the car while lightly pounding the baton in his fist.

The officer opened the back passenger side door and aggressively threw Seven out of the car on to the ground. He put his foot on Sevens back. "If you try to get away I'll put a bullet in your back," he speaks before removing the black backpack. He reached in the pockets of Seven and pulls out his cell phone. He places the phone in his right hand and throws it deep into the area of trees. Seven could see the phone land deep in area about 30 yards away from laying on his stomach. Seeing the phone flying through the air instantly discouraged the spirit of Seven. Knowing that his cell phone was the only way of contacting Destiny. The officer gripped his baton and raised it in the air aiming for the back of Seven. A light brush of wind began to shake the leaves on the trees. He paused right before swinging down. He was yet to swing although he had all intentions on doing so. He froze in swinging position and staring at the back of Sevens head. He lowered his baton and placed in its holster. Seven could hear the police officer draw his gun and remove the safety switch from behind him. "You better pray to your God there is money in this backpack." Seven closes his eyes and remains without a peep. He hears the officer unzip the backpack while still standing with one foot on Sevens back.

After hearing the officer unzip the backpack, there was a long pause. It was like birds stopped flying, the wind stop blowing, the trees stop flowing, and the cars from the distant road stopped moving. Silence and stillness was the sound of the officer who stood over Seven while staring into the backpack. The officer reaches into the bag and pulls out one of the health packet books. He looked at the faced down Seven, and then back at the book while realizing that Seven was the author of the book that read, written by: "I am your brother." Seven knew there wasn't any money inside, and so he closed his eyes and tightened his body up from not knowing if he was taking his last breath or not. The officer removed his foot from Sevens back and dropped the backpack to the ground. He dropped to his knees while still staring at the book and taking deep breaths with

Seven still laying faced down on the ground and his eyes closed.

OFFICER: There was a man I helped out by just doing my job. It was some time ago. I ran into him at a coffee shop in the neighborhood you live. And we spoke. He asked me about my wife and I told him that she was dying of cancer. She was in great pain. The chemo just made her worse. The treatments and all the medicines were supposedly keeping her alive. I ran out of money trying to keep her alive. I got myself in debt. And this is when I turned into a corrupt cop. That is when I began getting the money, by any means, in order to keep my wife alive. And this man gave me this very book to give to my wife. And so I did. And just as I was losing hope and spending long hours at work, she read this book. When I got home from work I would see this book by her bed side. And before my eyes, slowly but surely, month after month, she became better. I no longer had to spend so much money that we didn't have on fighting to keep her alive. She says this book is what saved her life.. why do you do it? What makes you do all of this for people who wouldn't do the same for you?

SEVEN: Because, I am your brother.

OFFICER: (Long pause) Well, I guess that explains it. I guess that kind of love does exist after all... You and Destiny have been cleared of all debt with the Northside boys and myself.

Seven feels the officer stick a key inside the handcuffs and unlock them. He removed the handcuffs from

Sevens wrist and stood him back up on his feet. He gets
back into his police car and drives off. Seven turns over
on his back and looks up at the sky. He lifted his hand
towards the heavens. He remained in that position for
a moment while thanking God.

Miles away Destiny sat alone on a bus getting ready to
take off to a new location. Her worry grew after each
time she called Seven with no answer. She tried talking
to the bus driver to wait another ten minutes before
leaving but he informed her that he could not wait any
longer. She began to worry herself sick from not being
with the man who was changing her life. Destiny
walked back to her seat and grabbed her bag, there was
no way she was leaving without Seven. Right before she
began to walk away from her seat, she noticed the man
who attempted to rape her on the party bus was outside
the bus. Destiny hears the bus door close and the
engine prepare for takeoff. The Northside guy standing
outside the bus looks around amongst the crowd. She
knew he was there looking for her. Right before the bus
began to slowly take off is when her and the Northside
guy made eye contact. He immediately began to take
off running towards the bus. He began shouting, "stop
this bus," while pounding the side of the moving bus.
The bus driver speaks, "sorry my man, we are behind
schedule and we gotta go." Destiny and the Northside
guy make eye contact while he continued to beat on the
bus where she stood staring back. The bus picked up
speed and drove away. A relief, but sadness all over

again for Destiny June. She instantly had regrets and wanting their getaway spot to be a surprise. She wished she would have just told him. Now he has no idea what part of the country she would be. She tries to call him again but now his phone was going straight to voicemail. Defeat and worry got the best of the now drained Destiny.

The only way Seven could get ahold of Destiny was by retrieving his phone. He lifted himself from the ground and looked in the direction where the officer threw his phone. He looked back towards the highway, then looked back towards the area his phone was at. Seven wasted no time and did whatever he had to do in order to find Destiny. A small phone being thrown in this big area of the unknown. He started from an area and dialed in at every inch near him. He moved slowly in the vicinity of the tossed phone, moving from left to right. He took a step forward and began to move from right to left. For hours Seven searched the area with no luck. When fatigue kicked in he thought of Destiny June and carried on with a new dose of energy and determination. He moved through trees, weaved through branches, focused through the mosquito bites, and crawled on his hands and knees. Hours passed with no water or food. He searched and searched until day light began to fade. His strength and awareness began to reduce. He crawled and patted parts of the ground. His clothes were stained with dirt marks smeared on his face. His fingernails filled with dirt, while sweat dripped from his face. His body ran out of gas while pushing through on fumes in the near pitch dark night. He pushed through when seeing doubles throughout his search. He kneeled down on his hands and knees with his head tilted down while asking God for strength. He stopped his search and lifted himself up while on his knees. He tilted his back while looking up towards the dark sky. He took off his backpack and placed it on the ground in front of him before falling face forward on the backpack and passed out.

Seven opened his eyes to daylight and to see a beetle crawling along the veins in his hand. Soon as he thought of Destiny he arose from the ground and began to walk towards the highway. People from inside their cars driving by might have thought Seven was homeless from all the dirt and grass stains on his clothes until it was the last person he would have thought to stop and help him. It was a white man with a cowboy hat on driving a big Texas pickup truck by the name of Cowboy Bill. He pulled up next to Seven who was walking on the side of the rode.

COWBOY BILL: (Heavy country accent) Howdy partner. Where ya headed to?

SEVEN: I thank you for stopping sir. The next stop where I can be picked up will do.

COWBOY BILL: Hop right in and I'll getcha there. Looks like ya had a rough night and need a little lift.

SEVEN: Yes, very long night. It's a long story, but I'm searching for the love of my life and she can be anywhere in the world.

COWBOY BILL: Oh I see. Well, I don't know the situation and all, and I ain't the sharpest tool in the shed, but usually the signs were right there in front of us. Let's say your ridin a bull right (lifts his hand in the air and begins moving it back and forth as if he was riding a bull) and you rope those signs with that instinct and it's hard to go wrong. I've been living here on earth for little over 53 years, and I've learned that what is meant to be, will happen.

A few more miles up the road and Cowboy Bill pulled over into a gas station. Seven really appreciated Bill. He was never one to judge, but it just surprised him that a man like Cowboy Bill would be so kind to help him out. Before shaking Bill's hand and getting out of his truck, Seven just had to ask the question.

SEVEN: Sir, I have to ask this question, what caused you to pull over and help me out?

COWBOY BILL: Well, to be honest, I really don't know what caused me to do that, cause I never do. Something just led me to pull over for some odd reason. And what's strange is, I never intended to come out this way. I actually missed my turn back yonder. I reckon your surprised an old white man like myself pulled over to help a man of color out.

SEVEN: Yes, it's rare, but definitely a breath of fresh air when running into people like yourself.

COWBOY BILL: I've grown to learn that, no matter the color or where ya from, we all bleed the same red blood. We all get up and go to work to provide for our families. Hell, were all in this thing together when you take a deeper look. It's unfortunate that a small percentage of people that give the rest a bad name. I didn't used to think this way. I had to unlearn what I was taught and getta hold of some understanding. And you'll gain a lot of understanding when your a high school head football coach and about 80 percent of my players are black. And I would be offended if any of them wouldn't consider me family. Cause I love 'em and treat them all like my own son. Once a man loses fear of what he doesn't understand, you'll see people and the world differently.

When Seven shook Bill's hand, Bill could feel the great amount of appreciation in Seven's eyes. When Seven turned and walked away from the truck, Cowboy Bill honked his horn and shouted, "happy 4th of July partner, YEEHAW," and drove off. Seven waved at old Bill. Seven went inside the store and took care of his business. He called Diego to come pick him up so he get all cleaned up. While Diego was on his way, Seven really thought about what Cowboy Bill told him far as the signs being right there in front of us. Diego would drive Seven back to his home so he could take a shower and eat. Once Seven was ready, he had Diego drop him off at the bus station.

Seven stood at the bus stop with just his black backpack. He would let people cut in front of him from being indecisive. He was trying to put himself in the mind of Destiny. He was clueless and had just about ran out money. Wherever he decided to go, that was probably going to be his home or place until he figured out his next move. He asked God to guide him as he walked up to the counter. "One bus ticket to coast of California please." The next bus to Cali was in three hours. He waited with a feel of uncertainty and disappointment within himself. The disappointment for not memorizing Destiny's phone number was evident from his facial expression. So many scenarios plagued his mind while waiting. Did she even make it to her destination from the Northside boys capturing her? What if she wasn't okay right now? What if she never took the bus from him not meeting up with her? Discouragement piled on the mind of Seven as he impatiently waited to get on the bus.

The stress caused Seven to sleep most of the way to California. Worry stole his appetite. The people sitting across from him could feel that he was dealing with a heavy heart. How could he allow this to happen is what he kept asking himself? Although, he remained having faith, but he couldn't fight the feel of defeat. Being optimistic would be putting on a front. If Destiny was not going to be there, he had no idea what he was going to do from there. All he had was the clothes he had on and enough money for food that would last a few days. Time passed and the 3rd rolled into the 4th of July.

The bus arrived in Los Angeles just before dark. He asked to be pointed in the direction of the beach. The backpacker traveled west. The closer to the coast he became, the more he recognized where he was at from his past visit. He weaved through the city and made his way down to the sandy beach. Fireworks began to light up the sky. Fireworks and the sound of the ocean was the song that played. He passed by people enjoying the fireworks while laying out on lawn chairs. Seven's eyes were locked straight ahead with only one thing on his mind, and that was Destiny June. The further he walked, the less people he began to see. His heart began to beat faster once spotting the beach house he hoped and prayed where she would be.

Seven approaches closer to the beach house. He can see the part right where he, Destiny, and King sat and talked. The very part of the ocean where King was baptized. His emotions ran deeper and deeper as he approached closer. He didn't know if his heart could take another defeat by Destiny not being there. The highs and lows of the past few days had been an emotional roller coaster for the seeker. He can see that there are no lights on in the beach house as he moves in closer. The fireworks that light up the sky from a distance caused the whole scene to look like a masterful painting. Seven stood there staring at the house trying to hold it together. He walks up the stairs that leads to the balcony. A sick feeling began to arrive in his body from sensing that nobody was home. He walks to the door and stands there for a moment. He takes a deep breath and then finally knocks. No answer. He waits for a moment, while wishing everything in his soul that the door would open and see his love. But still, there was no answer. He knocks again. No answer.

Seven turns and around and looks out into the ocean. He looks upwards to the sky and thinks how he just might have to accept his fate. He slowly walks back across the balcony and begins the longest walk down stairs. Once he made it down the stairs, he sees a stick laying in the sand and picks it up. He walks halfway towards the cool and calm ocean water, then turns around and stares at the home. He stood in between the ocean and a beach house. Seven began to use his stick to draw words in the sand. His anger caused him to dig a little deeper in the sand. He worked up a small sweat before drawing the last word. A draining feel of numbness for the young traveler. He took his shoes off and began to walk closer to the water while holding the stick in his hand.

The water washed up the shore, surrounding his feet as he stares out far as the ocean will go. He thinks to just keep on walking into the ocean and allowing the water to have its way with him. He lifts the hand that holds the stick and wipes the sweat from his forehead. He paused from smelling a familiar fragrance. He goes through the motion of wiping the sweat above his eye brow, and once again he smells that familiar scent. He thought maybe he was missing her so much that he could smell her. He leans forward a little and smells the stick just above his hand. He smells the stick once more. And it was so, the very scent of Destiny, the one he could never get tired of.

His eyes grew wide. Instant energy activated in his body. He turned around with a sense of hope and looked at the beach house from afar. And there she was, Destiny June slowly making her way to the edge of the balcony. They both locked eyes at a distance. The world around them became still. Only the music from the ocean played. With her eyes still locked on Seven, Destiny began to pat and feel around her to touch something physical, just to let her know that she wasn't in a dream. She felt the wooden post and her body weaken for a slight second. She put both of her hands over her face, just below her teary eyes. The expression on his face was as if God had sent an angel from heaven.

Destiny walks down the stairs and takes off running once she reaches the sand. Seven drops the stick in his hand, takes off his backpack, and began to run towards Destiny. Once they met half way near the writing in the sand, Destiny jumps into the arms of Seven and cries out, "yes, yes!" Seven lifts her up and she wraps her legs around his waist. From looking down from above, there was a beach house and the ocean, and in between was Destiny and Seven holding each other next to the words, "will you marry me," written in the sand. The different lights from the fireworks change the color of her tears of joy. He puts her back down and slowly takes one knee in the sand. He reaches down in his pocket and takes out a ring.

SEVEN: I felt like I was dying without you. It made me realize how much I am in love with you. I want to be with you forever. God molded me just for you, and you for me. Destiny June.. will you marry me?

DESTINY: My dreams have come true, for God to send me a man just like you. Yes, I will marry you.

Loud fireworks set off right after she says yes. Seven puts the ring on her finger. He stands to his feet and kisses the beautiful Destiny.

The afternoon was arriving in the next day, while the two love birds laid in bed together. The windows were open and the fresh breeze was felt. The sound of the waves brushing the shore played over and over.

DESTINY: How did you know to where to find me?

SEVEN: Before I had to make a decision on what bus to take. I ran into a man that stopped and helped me. And I told him I was searching for my love who could be anywhere. And he told me that the signs are usually right there in front of me and I began to remember you saying that being here at the beach house is your favorite place to be during 4th of July. I remember being here on the beach with you and King, and when I was writing, I felt a beach beetle crawl on my foot. I moved it off of me and watched it crawl closer to the most beautiful thing walking this earth, which happened to be you. When you couldn't reach me on my phone, that police officer with the eye patch threw my phone far away from me. And once he let me go from coming close to killing me, I searched for that phone the rest of the day and night until I passed out. The next morning, I was woken up by a beetle crawling on my hand. I connected that sign with asking God to guide me. And what do you know, I found my future wife.

DESTINY: (She checks the time) All the sacrifices it took for you to finally get me. And all the patience and discipline it took for me to finally get you. I'm so glad you found me. I know what it feels like to be dying inside, while still being alive. I thought something happened to you and I didn't know if I was ever going to see you again. I just cried until I couldn't cry no more. I cried myself to sleep right before the fireworks started. I was dreaming, and in my dream there were knocks at the door. The fireworks woke me out of my sleep. And the next moments after I woke up just happens to be the best moment of my life. I walk outside and see my angel standing there with my stick in his hand. I knew then, that everything was going to be alright.

SEVEN: What a classic scene that would be to the ending of a book.

DESTINY: (Looks at the time and rises up in the bed while facing Seven) I have a confession to make.

SEVEN: I'm all ears babe.

DESTINY: On the night you saved me and those guys jumped you, when you laid on the ground unconscious,

I hugged you, and when I did, I took your keys and wallet. And while you were at the hospital, King went to your apartment. And ever since he walked into your world is when he began to change. He already knew a lot about you before meeting you. He was only going to reward you for saving me, but once he felt like you were chosen, he felt like you both could have helped each other reach your mission and carry out each other's plan.

SEVEN: It's all starting to make more sense now. He knew what he wanted to do with all of that money from the jump (shaking his head in amazement). The brilliance of the King. Was it just me, or did King know that his time was coming to an end. And before that day happened, he mentioned little things to prepare us for that very day, as if he had this whole thing planned out?

DESTINY: Yes, I believe so. And yes, he knew what he wanted to do with the money. To give it all back. But he needed the right man for the job. And that is where you came in. And I also believe that he chose you for me as well. I think you were the only man he thought was good enough for me. He never brought it up, but I'm pretty sure he saw how I looked at you sometimes, or how my eyes gazed when he was giving me the run down on you. I asked him all kinds of questions when he was in your apartment. He told me what all he saw, from the writings, to the mail in your trash can. And so I took it upon myself to help out with something you were searching for (hopes she didn't overdo it). And, we both knew that you were going to run through that money from the goodness of your heart. Which brings me to a gift I have for you.

SEVEN: I got my gift, I got you. Well, I guess that makes two of us, because I have something for you as well.

They both lift up from the bed, destiny walks into the closet and comes back out with a show box while Seven walks over to pick up his black backpack.

DESTINY: I knew you were going to do great things with the money King left for you. And so I assumed you would have used it all up in order to complete your mission. So, I took all the money I made for the work vacation not too long ago and saved it all for you (Destiny opens the shoe box that was filled with stacks of money). And not to mention, I have been saving most of my money for some years, plus this money here.. babe we good!

SEVEN: (In aw of the money in the show box. He hugged her while thanking her) This feels too good to be true. What did I do to deserve everything in front of me right now? I guess in due time, we do reap what we sowed. Well, when I wasn't doing for the people back in home, I was working on the book about Destiny June and King. And early this morning while you were sleep, the ending that was blank became filled. (Opens his black backpack with several health packet books and pulls out the edited rough draft) Here is the story of my time with the great Destiny and King, but with different characters name. I hope you like it. I think it's going to be a number one best seller.

Seven hands Destiny the book and she receives it with a priceless joy. She stares at it for a moment before pressing it up against her chest. They both hug each other in pure happiness. Destiny looks at the time once again, right before there was a knock at the front door. Destiny looks into Seven's eyes.

SEVEN: Are you expecting someone?

DESTINY: Yes, it's the second surprise I have for you.

SEVEN: (While still holding Destiny) Oh is that right. How did you know that I was going to be here if I just showed up last night?

DESTINY: I was going off the original plan of us leaving together and being here. I already had the second surprise set up before leaving to Dallas. (The doorbell rings again) Can you get the door for me please?

She releases herself from his arms and drifts off to into the bathroom. Before entering the bathroom door, she turns around and smiles while watching him leave the room. Seven walks to the front door. He looks out the peep hole and sees on older man who seemed to be in his fifties. Seven opens the door and the two look at each other in their eyes. Then, the man speaks. Hello son, it's a pleasure to meet you. My name is Joe. Most people call me Info Joe.